HER EX'S SECRET

Her Ex's Secret

TRICIA SAXBY

Pete's Press

To Chris, Nicholas, and Clark
My Team Awesome

Chapter 1

"You're *sooo* close to being fired."

Karen Allen took the threat from her boss in her stride and bit her tongue to prevent any more words from tumbling past her tightly closed lips. When will she ever learn to keep her comments to herself? Her job didn't involve expressing her opinion. But then again, she didn't listen to herself that often either.

"You asked me what I thought of this scarf—"

"I was *not* talking to you."

Karen took a quick look around the room. "There's no one else here."

Natasha Vale, the legend behind the prestigious Vale Designs, swung her head to the side and lowered her chin, her eyes mere slits as she clenched and unclenched her hands. Anyone else in the fashion world who knew Natasha, a.k.a. the Dragon Lady of New York's fashion world, would have left the room and gone into hiding when she posed like that, but Karen stood her ground. After almost three months of putting up with Ms. Vale's bullying nature, she wasn't about to cave now.

"You never learn, do you, Kara?"

"It's Karen, and no."

Natasha's gaze drifted past Karen's shoulder, and her lips formed a small smirk. "Well, *Karen*, it seems your coworkers agree with me on that."

An intense heat shot up her neck and into her cheeks as she looked around and saw a few fellow employees she thought she had befriended standing around the water cooler snickering behind their coffee cups. Why did she always feel like she never belonged?

"Ha." Natasha's voice echoed across the room, and the fleeing girls took cover at their desks. "Tell me then, what is wrong with the scarf?"

Karen took the scarf from Natasha's hand and let it slip in and out of her fingers, allowing the fabric to caress her skin.

"The scarf is lovely and soft with an engaging blue hue, but it doesn't go with this new line you're proposing for Fashion Week."

Natasha closed the distance between them. "You are only an intern," she said. "What do you know about anything?"

Karen should've stepped back, but she didn't. If anything, she leaned closer, so the tips of their noses almost touched. "I've been doing this for a long time.

Maybe not for your eclectic fans, but for an audience nonetheless." *Her cat counted as an audience, right?*

Natasha let out a loud cackle. "You have an audience?"

"Yes." Karen refused to be bullied by this woman who caused people to scatter when she walked by. *What made her so much better than anyone else?*

"Excuse me?"

"What?" Karen said and stepped back.

"Do you really want me to answer that?"

Dammit. She'd done it again—spoken her thoughts out loud. "No." She hunched her shoulders with a deep sigh.

If she wasn't more careful, she'd be fired from her internship and could kiss the coveted designer assistant position goodbye. This alone was the reason she'd given up her job as a business administrator at *Dogwood* Magazine in Vancouver and moved to New York.

Natasha yanked the scarf from Karen's hand, swung it around her neck, and tied it with an expert precision. "If you want to make it in this business, Kara, you need to keep your mouth shut and agree with everything that is being said. Do you understand?"

"Yes...and it's Kar—"

"Go and get me a coffee and be snappy about it—before I change my mind about you."

Natasha power-walked out of her office, her three-inch heels sending out a staccato beat against the tile floor. Karen followed in her wake, snatched her purse and coat off her desk and made a hasty exit to the bustling street below.

»»·««

What on earth had he been thinking when he'd chosen to miss out on a drag race in Monte Carlo to be here? At least the parade of beautiful women he'd be in close contact with during Fashion Week would stroke his ego and keep him busy. He could even dump Mindy, his current red-haired beauty, for a new model.

"Leo, darling. What about this one?"

Leopold St. Clare glanced at the sapphire bracelet donning the girl's wrist. "Wonderful. Shall we get it?"

Mindy jumped up and down and squealed her delight. "Pretty please."

Normally, Leo would have gotten a kick out of her pleasure over shiny, expensive jewelry, as it always led to great bed sport, but lately he'd been bored with her. Hell, with *everything*.

It only took a moment before they were back on the sidewalk with the brisk winter wind howling around them. All things considered, it felt good to be back in the Big Apple. He could have done without the cold. He'd been enjoying his estate in Tuscany when he'd received a phone call from an old friend offering him a gig during Fashion Week in New York.

Well, why the hell not? He hadn't been to the States in months, and again he'd noticed a deep unsettling in his circumstances. He knew part of his discontentment had to do with his parents constantly being on his case about the family business...but mostly he missed his sister.

Needing to escape his daily routine and the ever-familiar surroundings, he'd had his private jet ready within the hour and an excited Mindy along for the ride. And now, what he'd hoped would have fixed his discontentment seemed to be worse.

"Leo?"

"Yes?"

"It's cold. Can we head back to the condo now?"

"Of course." She'd gotten what she wanted. Now it was time for her to return the favour.

His limo waited for them across the street. Rushing to join the pedestrians as they crossed at the intersection, Leo slipped his arm around Mindy's waist and guided her through the throng of people. A woman headed straight for them, head down, concentrating on not spilling the coffee in her left hand or dropping the dry-cleaning bag in her right. The light changed colour and car horns from each direction blared, but the woman didn't look up. She didn't pick up her pace either.

Impatient drivers inched their way through the intersection, not caring about the pedestrians. Out of the corner of his eye, he saw a motorcycle zigzagging between lanes and cars, determined to make it through before the light changed. His conscience played tug-of-war between the thought of pushing the woman off the street, and screaming at her for being so unaware of her surroundings, or escorting her to safety like a true gentleman.

The man on the motorcycle pressed his horn insistently and waved his free arm in the air, but still no reaction. She must be on another planet.

Leo's adrenaline kicked into high gear, as it did before the start of a drag race. It ran through his veins like espresso and gave him a high he'd become addicted to. With no time to think, he pushed Mindy onto the sidewalk, spun around, and took a giant step toward the woman. He grabbed onto her wrist and yanked her to his chest. She let out a scream as the coffee spilled on the ground between them, both their clothes now stained. Traffic resumed its normal flow, and Leo's adrenaline rush crashed to join the coffee puddle. The idiot on the motorbike had no idea how close he'd come to injuring them both.

"What the hell! Why did you do that?" she shouted, but her focus remained on her coffee-stained clothes and the dry cleaning that had fallen into the dirty slush at the sidewalk's edge.

"I saved your life."

"Hmph. I doubt that. What you did was cost me my job."

"Who cares about a job more than a life?" The woman's stupidity continued to perplex him. What he needed to do was walk away, grab Mindy, and get to his limo for a preview of what would be happening once they reached his condo.

The woman scrubbed at the dry-cleaned clothing the flimsy bag hadn't protected, but to no avail, so she changed focus and started scrubbing dirt and snow off her pants. "You obviously must be new in town or you'd know my life was in no danger. You'll soon learn that, as impatient and annoying as some drivers are, they'd never hit someone."

"And you must be from Mars, because people here on Earth are selfish, are always in a hurry, and don't care one iota for your safety."

"You're a very negative person," she said.

Leo had had enough. If he was going to argue with someone, he wanted to look her in the eyes. Grabbing her by the chin with his index finger and thumb, he tugged her face upward. Bright green eyes met his, and he staggered back. His breath hitched as if the wind had been knocked out of him.

"Karen?" he said as his pulse roared in his ears.

He could see confusion mixed in with the anger in her expression, but as her eyes turned to a dark green, he knew in a moment that she recognized him.

"Leo?"

He desperately wanted to hug her and confirm that she was all right. So many years had passed since he'd last seen her...and what a knockout she'd grown into. Instead, he let his annoyance surpass all other emotion.

"What the hell is the matter with you?" he blurted out.

"I'm sure I already asked you that," she blurted back.

Leo let out a pent-up breath and glanced around them. How could anyone live amongst all this chaos of never-ending people, noise pollution, and cold? "Come. Let's get out of here."

"I'm not going anywhere with...you," she stammered after looking up at his face. He needed to work on keeping a more neutral expression. His poker face had never worked with this woman.

"Don't be ridiculous." He grabbed her elbow to pull her along the sidewalk to a free bench he'd spotted, but she didn't budge. "Bloody hell, Karen. Come on."

"I'm quite capable of walking all by myself, thank you very much." She tugged her elbow out of his grasp. The warm, tingly connection he'd felt through her thin jacket was lost. He wanted it back.

"We need to get off the street corner and somewhere safe."

"I need to get my boss a new coffee and drop off her dry cleaning."

"What exactly do you do?" Such menial tasks were below what he remembered Karen tolerating. They'd attended Simon Fraser University in Vancouver together, her working toward her business degree and him with his miscellaneous classes, since he could never decide what he wanted to do with his life. Back then the most important thing had been acquiring distance from his family and distraction from his problems back home.

He'd met Karen in their sophomore year, and a friendship had started instantly with their mutual dislike for their stats professor. It hadn't taken long before they were joined at the hip. She'd been such a breath of fresh air, so down to earth, and not like the other girls who were only there to party and who befriended him for his money.

"I'm interning for a fashion designer, but that doesn't matter now. I won't be for long when my boss finds out what happened."

"What happened was not your fault. What kind of boss would fire you because you spilled her coffee?"

"And dropped her cashmere dress in the mud."

His plan to keep her talking worked like a charm as he guided her toward the bench. "Here, sit down."

"What? Oh, okay."

Leo sat beside her, and the warmth he'd felt earlier filled him. He gazed at her blatantly like he'd been thirsty his whole life and was finally allowed to drink. She wore a pair of black leggings with tall tan boots and a thin black jacket. Her long blonde hair flowed in waves down her back, and her green eyes lit up like emeralds in a display case. Her smooth skin shone with vitality and youth. His fingers still tingled from touching her chin.

"How long have you been living in New York?"

"Umm...a few months." She hovered on the edge of the bench and glanced up and down the street, checking her watch every other second.

"And what brought you here?"

"Fashion."

"You're quite the conversationalist."

Karen stood and clutched the cashmere dress close to her chest. "I'm really sorry, Leo. I need to go."

Was this job really that important to her? The Karen he remembered didn't do anyone's bidding. But he'd enjoyed making her bend to his.

"Can I escort you?" he asked as he stood. The closeness sent his senses into a whirlwind.

"Leo? Darling?"

Shit. He'd forgotten all about Mindy. She ran with tiny steps toward him and wedged herself between him and Karen, pushing Karen out of the way. Leo's arm automatically wrapped around Mindy's waist as she planted a big wet kiss on his lips.

"Don't worry about it. Looks like you have your hands full."

Karen turned away and headed in the direction she'd come from. His gaze never left her slim form as she crossed the street and disappeared in the throng of people. A deep ache formed in his gut, but he kept a tight smile on his face as he led Mindy to the limousine.

»»·««

"Natasha is furious," Stacey, Natasha's personal assistant, announced as Karen dashed to her desk with a fresh coffee but no dry cleaning. "Where's her dress? She needs that for tonight."

Oh no! Panic started its wiggly dance in Karen's stomach. She took three deep breaths, squared her shoulders, and grabbed the coffee. Time to face the wrath of Ms. Vale. She rapped her knuckles on the door three times and waited.

"Come in."

Karen rubbed her free hand down the length of her thigh before grabbing the doorknob and letting herself in.

"Here's your coffee, Ms. Vale."

"Excellent. I do hope it's to my exact liking."

"Black with two creams."

"One cream." Natasha clucked her tongue then sighed. "My dear Kara. I have high expectations for my interns—"

"It's Karen, and for the past three months it's been with two creams."

Natasha stood, sending her chair rolling away. "Is your mind so minuscule that you've already forgotten the advice I gave you earlier?"

Karen lifted her chin in defiance. Normally, if anyone talked to her like that, she'd have decked them and joined them on the floor for a good old catfight.

"Well?"

"You told me to keep my mouth shut and do what I'm told, but how I am supposed to do that when you keep changing your mind?"

"I need an intern who can transition to the changes I need to make on a moment's notice. I definitely do not need a wannabe who can't even get a coffee order correct."

Karen silently chanted her daily mantra. *I need to finish this internship.* This was her door into the elite fashion world of New York. True, this was an adventure she'd wanted to have with her bestie, Anna Marlow, who was in the process of designing her own clothing line. Now a newlywed with a baby on the way, Anna had to stay in Vancouver, which had put their shared dream on hold. So, Karen had taken this solo opportunity to intern at Vale Designs and fulfill her dream of turning her design hobby into a career. With her background in business, her position at *Dogwood Magazine* hadn't given her any time to explore her love for designing, but Karen had soaked up everything she could watching Anna work her magic over the years.

Unfortunately, interning for Natasha Vale for the past three months had brought her no closer to her dream, and holding her tongue had proven to be difficult. Not as difficult as pretending she knew nothing about the fashion industry, though.

"You're right," Karen said. "I apologize." *Oh, that was hard.*

"Hmm." Natasha reached for her eyeglasses, which were perched on top of her head. When she put them on, her already large eyes grew to remind Karen of an owl.

"What on earth happened to your clothes?" She took a step closer to Karen and let her gaze drag up and down her body. Karen wanted to cringe. "You're covered in mud, and you smell like...coffee."

"I...umm, well..." Her stomach rebelled with her anxiety.

"Spit it out already."

"There was an incident at the crosswalk."

"An incident?"

"Yes. I had your coffee and dress, and there was a guy on a motorbike who wouldn't stop..."

"My dress? Where is it?"

"At the dry cleaners."

"It was due for pickup today."

"Yes."

"And?"

Karen thought she might vomit. The butterflies that had plagued her since she'd entered Natasha's office tripled in agitation, rising to her throat. That cashmere dress was Natasha's favorite. Mud and coffee came out of white cashmere, right?

"Well, I had to take it back to the dry cleaners. It...there was some..."

"Unbelievable," Natasha snapped.

"It's only a dress."

"Only a...only a...dress," Natasha repeated, her breaths shallow and fast.

"I'm sure it will be fine. Richard can work miracles."

"Yes. Miracles." Natasha sat and leaned back in her chair. *Always the drama queen*, Karen thought. "Tell me. Which cashmere dress was it?"

Karen's eyebrows knit in question. "Stacey said you'd be wearing it tonight at the opening gala."

"The black one? Please tell me it was the black one. Yes, Richard can get anything out of black cashmere."

Oh, how Karen wished she were the fainting type. That would be the perfect escape to such a crazy, disastrous day.

"Well?" Natasha screeched at her. "I'm quite sure you know what colour my dress is."

"It wasn't the black one."

"That leaves...my white one."

Karen rushed to explain. "Yes, but it barely had anything on it. You won't even know."

"I'll know."

"No. It'll be fine. I promise."

"It better be fine or you'll owe me a thousand dollars."

A thousand dollars? She couldn't afford that. She wasn't getting paid for this internship, and her roommate wasn't going to let her bum off him forever. She would have gotten a second job if there were more hours in a day, but right now she was lucky if she got home before ten o'clock each night. Even free weekends were sparse with the ramp-up for Fashion Week.

"When will my dress be ready?" Natasha asked, her voice continuing in an eerie monotone.

"I put a rush on it, so it should be ready by five o'clock."

"At cost to the company?"

Yes, but she wasn't about to tell her that. "No. I'll cover it."

"Good." She lifted her coffee cup to her lips and took a long sip. "My coffee is ice cold. Go and get me a new one. Two creams."

Before Karen voiced her opinion again, she left as fast as she could, avoiding Stacey's questions and the piercing stares of the other interns. As she rode the elevator down to the lobby, her thoughts continued to swirl. She had to get it right this time. One compliment from this witch woman would make this whole situation so much more bearable.

The elevator doors chimed and opened to let her out. With a game plan in place, she decided this time she'd get two coffees and *cover her ass.*

"And it's quite a nice ass you have too."

Karen stopped short and turned. Reclining on one of the lobby couches was Leo—all six foot two of the dark-haired, muscled, gorgeous playboy who only had to blink and anything he wanted was his.

"What are you doing here, Leo? I thought you were with your redhead."

He stood and reached her side in two long strides, causing her pulse to race. "I had my driver take her back to the condo. I'm here to see you." No beating around the bush with this guy. She'd always liked that about him.

His condo? A dull ache filled her chest, and she silently scolded herself. What did she care? He could do whatever he wanted with whomever he wanted. "I don't have time to chat." She headed to the lobby door, which the doorman opened for her.

"Whoa. Hold up, Karen." Leo caught up with her on the sidewalk. He touched her elbow, and a hot burst of lust zoomed to her groin.

"I need to get my boss more coffee."

His golden eyes, which had acquired him the nickname "The Golden Lion" back in college, turned dark amber. "Seriously?"

"Don't even get me started." Karen turned away from Leo and picked up her walking pace. She didn't have time to make small chat with an old flame. Well, "old flame" according to her, anyway. Leo had never had the time of day for her after that one night.

"Can I tag along?" he asked as he kept pace with her long strides.

"I'd prefer if you didn't."

"I'm great company."

Karen didn't doubt that. Checking her watch, she groaned. How on earth had so much time slipped away? She veered to the left and dashed across the street. People yelled and honked their horns, but she didn't care.

"Next time tell me before you do something stupid like that," Leo said when he caught up to her. He wasn't even a bit winded from the jog.

"I'm not here to entertain you. I have an errand to run, and if I don't get it right this time, I'll be fired for sure."

"Over coffee?"

"Over her expensive white cashmere dress being covered in coffee and mud stains."

"I'm sure she can purchase another one."

"She most definitely could, but I'm not about to be the one to tell her that." Not after everything else she'd said.

"I'm assuming you took it back to the dry cleaners."

"Yes, and I put a rush on it." They crossed another intersection and headed to the corner coffee shop. "She needs it for tonight's gala."

"What gala?"

Karen stopped and opened the coffee shop door, inhaling deeply. She loved the smell of fresh ground coffee beans.

"You know there are half a dozen coffee shops on the same block as your building."

"Yes, but this is where she gets her coffee. Every day."

"Nothing like trying something new," Leo mumbled, and he sat on a stool as Karen placed her order.

"Want anything?"

"No."

Once she had a cup of coffee in each hand, Karen said goodbye to Leo and made her way back to work hurriedly.

"You still haven't told me about the gala."

"I thought you'd left," Karen said with a sigh. He was becoming quite a nuisance. "What are you doing here anyway?"

"I asked a question first." He snatched one of the coffees out of her hand and kept walking.

"Right, the gala." Karen had to increase her stride to keep up with him now. "Next week is Fashion Week, and this gala is the kick-off for all the activities that will be happening in the downtown core."

"And are you, the most prized intern, invited to this fancy gala?"

"Not a chance. I'm only the most prized intern."

They had slowed down, and Leo was staring at her, a huge grin on his face.

"What?"

"I always enjoyed your dry humor. I've missed it."

Karen wanted to grab onto the compliment and run. How dire were her circumstances that she yearned for praise from anyone who'd give it? This particular someone being a mistake from the past...but she wasn't in a position to be picky.

"Thanks." She tilted her head and returned his grin.

"You haven't changed a bit." Leo's voice held a soft rumble that had goosebumps racing down her arms. A gust of wind whipped around them as they stood facing each other on the sidewalk. She laughed, the sound a light tinkling as her scarf billowed between them.

"Oh yes, I've changed. It's been five years, and you know nothing about me now."

"I want to."

Karen shoved him aside. "I'm not going to do this with you."

"Do what?"

"You have a girlfriend. A beautiful redhead who most likely is a model here for Fashion Week. Am I right?"

Leo shrugged. "I wouldn't call her my girlfriend, but yes, she's a model."

They reached her destination, and she extended her hand out for the coffee he held. "Please."

His full, sensuous lips crept up at the corners and his golden eyes lit up with humour. "You say that so nicely."

"Behave yourself." The last thing she needed was this man to cause uncontrollable butterflies in her stomach. She'd been there, done that with him, and it had led to heartache. She could not go there again.

Leo took a sip of the coffee and scrunched his face in disgust. "Ugh, no sugar."

Karen almost dropped the cup she held. "What are you doing? That coffee is for—"

"Your boss. I know, I know."

"Give it to me."

"I'd love to, but now's not the time."

Karen rolled her eyes. "Are you for real?"

"I wouldn't lie about something like that."

Karen frowned. "I don't have time for this."

"I'll see you to your desk."

"That's not necessary."

"It's not, but you need help carrying this cup of coffee."

A short burst of laughter escaped from her lips. Now she remembered why they'd gotten along so well. That and the sexual tension they could keep at a constant low burn.

"Fine, but I'm warning you, she's got quite the temper. She'll definitely know we did something to her precious coffee."

"Yours is still untouched."

"And it'll stay that way," she said, and she brought the cup close to her chest.

They rode the elevator to the top floor in silence. She thanked her lucky stars it was a fast ride. When the doors opened, Karen stepped out and then stopped short. Natasha was standing in the middle of the foyer, her legs shoulder width apart and her hands on her hips, an unflattering grimace making her look clown-like.

"Did you go to Brooklyn for my damn coffee?"

"May as well have." She held the cup out to Natasha, who grasped it so hard the lid popped off and sent creamy liquid to splash on Karen's boots and the newly waxed marble floor.

"Look what you've done." Natasha screeched.

"I've done nothing. You're the one—"

A loud throat-clearing sound came from behind her. "Excuse me, ladies."

"What?" Karen and Natasha snapped, their focus on the sudden distraction.

"Can I offer my assistance?"

Karen faced Natasha; whose mouth formed a perfect "O".

After what felt like an eternity, Natasha turned to Karen with a smile. "Kara, meet our new Fashion Week photographer, Leopold St. Clare."

Chapter 2

So, this was what it felt like to be hit by a train…or at least what Karen figured it would feel like. The tightness in her chest and the high-pitched buzzing in her ears accompanied the heavy sensation in her limbs, making it impossible to move. She hadn't heard correctly. Leo wasn't the new photographer. None of this made sense. Leo was a playboy to the highest extreme. Living the life on his Tuscany estate, a girl on each arm and wine from his family's vineyards flowing like water. What did Leo know about fashion or taking pictures…or working?

She had to say something. Anything was better than standing here looking like a gulping fish.

You've gotta be kidding me.

The annoyed glare from Leo and exasperated sigh from Natasha told her quite clearly that she'd opened her big mouth without thinking first…again.

"You know better than anyone that I don't kid around." Natasha brushed at the air as if swatting a pesky fly. "Now get back to work. I've left you a pile of paperwork to file."

Touching Leo's elbow, she guided him down the hall and into her office. The door slammed shut behind them, and Karen let out a big whoosh of air.

"Who was that?" Stacey asked, eyes-popping cartoonishly.

Karen refused to answer as she made her way past the swooning spectacle to her desk. True to her word, Natasha had literally piled her desk with papers. Payback, no doubt.

She mindlessly sorted through the first pile and alphabetized it for filing. Why hadn't he told her they'd be working at the same company? He knew that she worked for Natasha Vale. He'd gotten an earful during the whole coffee-and-dress disaster...or had he?

Karen stopped shuffling the papers in her hands and placed them gently on the pile she'd pulled them from. No, he wouldn't have known. She'd only referred to her as "boss," and really, that could have been anyone.

It came down to the fact that he hadn't asked, and she hadn't told.

She recalled how he'd come to her rescue in the foyer before she'd embarrassed herself even more in front of her co-workers. Twice now Leo St. Clare had come to her rescue.

She didn't like it one bit. She wasn't some fairy tale princess who needed her Prince Charming to come riding in on his steed and make everything perfect. She didn't want it to be either.

Her phone buzzed with an incoming text. Natasha's dress was ready. Releasing a sigh of relief, Karen grabbed her jacket and purse and left before someone else could give her an errand to do.

A burst of cold air hit her as she stepped onto the sidewalk. Pulling her jacket tighter, she bent against the bitter wind and power-walked to the dry cleaners. Glancing up from time to time, she saw more frowns than happy faces in the throng of people that filled the sidewalk. With the Christmas rush long gone and New Year celebrations done for another year, all that was left were bitter weeks of cold and what Karen liked to call the February blahs.

Since moving to New York, she'd had a real wake-up call. She wasn't in small-town Oak Valley, British Columbia, anymore. When she'd arrived at the end of fall, the leaves had been red and gold, the flower beds full of marigolds had still been vibrant, and pedestrians had been smiling. Happiness had oozed from everywhere, even the buildings. It'd been everything she'd hoped and wished for in this city of dreams. But that illusion had ended before that first day was done. She'd scoured the pavement looking for an apartment to rent. Nothing in her price range had been habitable, each place worse than the last, and all of them were run down and dark, with stained floors, filthy bathrooms, and cockroaches in the kitchen.

As the days stretched on, a fear she'd never known before took hold as desperation sank in. She'd been a fool to come here without doing research on housing first. She'd been determined to make it on her own with no help—and she'd failed. Grudgingly, Karen had called up an old friend who lived nearby and asked if she could crash with him until something better came along. Having to rely on others didn't sit well with her. She didn't want to be helped.

"Rescued" is more like it, Karen clarified to herself as she turned the corner and arrived at her destination. She opened the heavy door. Chimes announced her arrival, and Richard, famous tailor to the stars, popped up from behind the counter.

"Ah, Ms. Allen. You are quite prompt."

"You know who I work for."

Richard smiled and took her hand. "Do not worry, darling. I worked my miracle, and the dress looks better than it did before."

Karen let out a big breath she didn't know she'd been holding. "You are my hero."

"Indeed, I am," he said with a smirk as he shrugged.

Karen chuckled and a warmth filled her. "I owe you for that too."

Richard's eyebrows furrowed. "For laughter?"

"I'm afraid so." How depressing was that? When was the last time she'd laughed like that? *Earlier today with Leo,* she realised with a slight frown.

Richard passed her the dress, which was wrapped in a plastic zippered bag this time.

"Thank you. Oh, and you'd better charge it to me. Ms. Vale doesn't want to see it on the company books."

"Let me tell you what, darling. This time it is on the house."

Oh crap. Was he taking pity on her? That was the last thing she needed.

"I can afford it," she lied and averted her eyes. She didn't do well with handouts. Asking her friend for a place to live had been bad enough. It had been that or sleeping with the cockroaches. She'd come to terms with it and refused to accept help from anyone else since.

Richard rounded the counter and stood in front of her. "I do not doubt it, but you will accept my kindness."

She couldn't argue with a clothes genius. She smiled. "I will. I didn't mean to offend. Thank you, Richard."

Richard leaned forward and placed a kiss on each cheek. "You are welcome, darling." He released her and waved her away. "I will see you again soon."

"Most definitely."

Before the door slammed shut behind her, he called out, "And stay away from the coffee shop until after the dress has been delivered."

It was five thirty when she got back to work. Natasha's office door was wide open, so Karen entered and draped the dress over a chair where she'd be sure to see it.

"Well?"

Karen let out a yelp and her hand went to her throat. Her pulse beat rapidly beneath her fingers. "Ms. Vale?"

Natasha stepped through a gap in the navy-blue curtains that draped the floor-to-ceiling windows and walked into the room. "Well?" she repeated.

"I haven't looked at it." *Steady, pulse. Steady...*

"Then how—?"

"Richard told me it looks better than it did before. I trust him." Confidence flowed through her at Natasha's look of astonishment.

"Yes. Well, as do I."

"Right," Karen said as Natasha unzipped the bag and pulled out the dress. She turned it slowly, inspecting each side with her eagle-eyed gaze.

"Well, I'm done for the day."

"Yes, yes." Natasha waved her hand as if to brush her away. "Go."

Would it be so hard for her to utter some thanks? Karen thought. Oh, who was she kidding? It would have been too hard for the almighty Ms. Vale to thank anyone for anything.

Karen stopped at the door and turned around. "Have fun at the gala." *Was she a sucker for punishment?*

Natasha looked her in the eyes and smiled. "I intend to. Who wouldn't with Mr. St. Clare as an escort?"

Karen nodded and pretty much ran to the elevator.

Leo was taking Natasha to the opening gala. The one she wasn't good enough to attend after three months of working her tail off for the most impossible woman on the planet. And all he'd done was walk into Natasha's office for an hour and he was in. The supposed photographer. The playboy who could make the world bow to his bidding.

Anger seethed through her as she dashed through the lobby, ignoring the doorman's smile and nod as he held the door for her. The bitter wind greeted her, but she didn't zip up her coat or cover her head with the fashionable scarf Anna had made for her as a going-away present. The cold sting soothed her heated skin as she started to pick up speed. She made it to the corner before colliding with a solid wall of muscle.

Karen looked up to see Leo staring down at her, his golden eyes flashing with concern. Her heart beat wildly as a memory of them rolling around in his dorm bed flew to the forefront of her mind.

"What on earth? What are you doing?" He wrapped his arm around her and led her to shelter under a store canopy.

Why did he continue to be such a...gentleman? "I...I...need to get home. I have a busy night." Her teeth chattered like castanets when he removed his arm.

"Where is your house? Are you walking?"

"That is none of your business," she spat, and she made to leave, but Leo grabbed her hand and pulled her back.

"Did you and Natasha fight again?"

He was on a first-name basis with her now. *Unbelievable.* "No, I didn't get into a fight with my boss."

Leo stepped closer to block the wind that howled around them. When he spoke, his voice softened. "What's got you all bothered?"

Wouldn't he like to know? His huge ego would have gotten a great boost.

"Look, it's been a rotten day. I want to get home, have a nice, hot bath, and curl up with a good book."

What did she see swirling in his gaze? Desire? She heard his short intake of breath before he lowered his head to hers. "I want to kiss you so badly," he breathed.

I want to kiss you too... What? No, no, no. She wasn't going down that road again. Besides, who kissed one woman then took another on a date a few hours later? Leo St. Clare did.

Karen placed her hand on his chest and pushed him away. "You're feeling reminiscent. I get it. But I'm sure you'll have many chances to get your kisses and more tonight."

Leo's gaze intensified and then turned cold as a bright light flashed behind them.

"Hey, Mr. St. Clare. Who's the new beauty? Will you be taking her to the gala tonight?"

Blinding white lights left black spots floating in front of her eyes. "What's going on? Who was that?"

Leo did his best to shield her but to no avail. The camera was almost in her face now, and panic started to turn in her belly.

"Come on." He barreled through the gathering crowd of gawkers, pulling Karen along as fast as he could. They headed for the street, cars honking their horns as they weaved between them and made it to the other side unscathed.

"That's the last time you can give me advice about crossing the street."

"Deal."

A limo pulled up next to them, and Leo opened the door and urged her inside. She scooted over so he could follow. The limo pulled away from the curb and joined the fast-moving traffic.

Adrenaline and excitement emanated off him in waves. "Where do you live? I'll get Robert to take us there."

The last thing she needed was Leo knowing where she lived. "Drop me off at the nearest subway entrance. I'll be fine."

The look he sent her created butterflies in her stomach.

"Where do you live?" he repeated.

Nope, not going to happen. "Leo, what the hell is going on? Why was that guy asking about me?"

"Paparazzo," he said as his gaze swept over her body, causing a flood of heat to rush down to her toes.

He was that popular? *Holy crap.* Definitely not her cup of tea. Imagine trying to have any kind of private life. But wasn't that the road she and Anna were trying to gear up for?

"How did he find you?"

"Well, I'm not exactly sure, but I'm guessing someone in the Vale Designs office."

Karen took instant offence. "Well, it wasn't me."

"I didn't think so."

"Besides, no one else knew who you were except my boss."

Leo leaned back and crossed his legs at the ankles. The half grin he flashed her sent a ripple of awareness through her. "For someone who doesn't like her job—"

"I like my job."

"Then for someone who doesn't like the people she works with, you sure are quick to come to their defence."

"I like my coworkers. My boss is another story."

"Ah, so you're not defending Ms. Vale?"

"Hell no."

Leo belted out a boisterous laugh. "Is she the culprit then?"

"Wouldn't put it past her. She wants the publicity as much for herself as for her clothing line."

"Such is life in the fashion industry, I'm afraid."

Karen nodded and turned her attention to the view outside. It appeared Robert was driving in circles, as the same downtown buildings passed by. And the one question, or maybe the one accusation she had, itched to be said out loud.

"You're going to the gala with my boss." Her shoulders tensed as she continued to watch the scenery. She didn't want to see the look on his face.

Leo grunted. "So that's what has your back up. I thought you didn't care."

Karen spun to face him. "I don't care."

"Liar," he said. Her cheeks burned under his gaze.

So much for him feeling any sort of guilt. Oh, who was she kidding? He had an in with the boss. Why wouldn't he milk it for all it was worth?

Feeling claustrophobic, and disgusted at having been rescued yet again, Karen knocked on the separation window to get Robert's attention. "You can let me off here."

Robert pulled the limo over, and Karen wasted no time opening the door and stepping out. She crouched a bit to say good-bye and saw a fearful scowl on Leo's face. *Good.* "I appreciated the company today. Have fun tonight."

Her smile didn't quite reach her eyes as she shut the door. The tinted window kept her from seeing his response, if any.

You did the right thing. She repeated this mantra as she walked toward the subway station...but didn't believe a single word.

»»·««

Morning had come too soon. With a large cup of coffee warming his hands, Leo leaned back against the limo's soft leather seats and closed his eyes, willing his headache to go away. He'd instructed Robert to get him to Vale Designs as fast as possible. He was late.

Who on earth had planned a photo shoot for the morning after the opening gala?

He'd had fun. It had been a great party but so superficial. The too-skinny models had worn outrageous outfits, with feathers being the theme of the night. Bright-coloured peacocks on display. The men had been no better, in makeshift suits and tuxedos with pant legs too short and shirts left untucked. Did no one wear the classics anymore? If preferring jeans and a T-shirt for casual and dressing up like James Bond for fancy nights out made him unstylish then so be it.

Perhaps his nonchalant approach to fashion made his photography so unique. Enough to get Natasha Vale to notice and hire him.

Taking a sip of the steaming hot java, he enjoyed the combination of creamy bitterness on his tongue as he looked out the window at the scenery that zipped by. Natasha had been all business when the evening had started. They'd circled the room for introductions then taken their front-row seats to the fashion show that sported some of Natasha's pieces. He'd instantly taken notice of a scarf—a blue-green shimmery mess. And he grimaced.

"What is it?" Natasha had asked.

"That blue-green scarf. It doesn't fit that look at all. I want to go up there and rip it off."

"Well, fuck."

"You didn't approve that, did you?"

"She told me," Natasha had said under her breath.

"What?"

"My newest intern, Kara. She said the same thing you did. I took offence. Who is she to say anything to me about fashion?"

Kara? "You mean Karen?"

Natasha had fluttered her hand in front of her face. "Yes, yes, whatever."

"You're angry she knew something you didn't."

"No—"

"Then why did you take offence to Karen's suggestion? Did you not hire her?"

"Not personally..."

"But someone in your company was impressed with her experience, meaning you'd be impressed. So, tell me again, what problem do you have with Karen?"

Natasha had faced him so abruptly, the model who was walking down the catwalk had jumped back and burst into tears. He'd waved her on with his hand before giving Natasha his undivided attention.

"The problem I have with Kara—"

"Nat, her name is Karen."

"I know."

"Then what?"

"She doesn't belong here."

Just then, the limo came to a sudden stop, jolting Leo out of his reminiscence.

"We're here, Mr. St. Clare."

"Thank you, Robert." Leo swung the door open and stepped onto the sidewalk. The usual midday chaos of endless people going somewhere greeted him and put his already frazzled nerves on edge. Taking a deep breath, he entered the building for his first swimsuit photo shoot, a favour for Nat.

Hoping for the same adrenaline rush he craved when racing, Leo entered the Vale Designs foyer from the elevator and absorbed his surroundings. The chaos from outside had spilled inside. Lights, umbrella deflectors, backdrops, stages, and racks of clothing filled up one part of the space. The rest was taken up by makeshift makeup stations, a buffet of salads and fruits, and then the many stylists, each catering to a starved model.

It wasn't until his gaze settled on Karen that his heart raced. She was trying to get a corset tied up on a model who looked like she'd snap in two if the corset were any tighter.

"It's good enough," the model gasped in between tugs of material.

Karen was out of breath as well. "It's never good enough. You know better."

Interesting thing to say, especially when Karen's voice lacked lustre. What was her role here as Natasha's intern? Not a morale booster, apparently.

"May I help?"

Karen turned at his question. Her eyes lit up with joy, but then it was gone. Imagined. "Oh. You finally decided to join us."

"Better late than never." His smile disappeared at her void stare.

"Ms. Allen?" the red-haired model moaned.

"It needs to be tighter."

"What on earth are you making her wear? A condom?"

Karen's lips turned up slightly at the corners. "Oh, something way worse."

The girl already appeared too pale and now looked positively grey. "What is it?"

"The nude suit."

Leo's brows arched with surprise. "Excuse me?"

Karen huffed her frustration before handing the corset's ribbons to him. "Make this as tight as you can. I'll be right back."

He watched her go. The natural sway of her backside had him thinking of all the wonderful things he'd love—

"Owww." He'd forgotten he had the silk strings in his hands.

"Sorry. Are you okay? Here, let me loosen that a bit."

Where on earth had Karen gone? Better question: where was he supposed to be?

"Mr. St. Clare?"

"Yes?"

A young woman with a brown ponytail and glasses ran toward him. "Did you want to take some sample shots before we start?"

"That'd be great. Thanks."

The girl's cheeks lit up to a bright pink. "Okay. Follow me."

He had a nice little set-up in the far corner of the studio. The backdrop was of a beautiful Hawaiian beach. It was a far cry from the real thing, but it'd do. He'd have the models standing and maybe lying on a towel. And props—he needed props. Sun hats, sunglasses, wraps, strappy sandals...

"A romance novel."

He knew it was her, and the realisation she was standing behind him had a rush of pure lust running through him.

"Do you have one to recommend?"

"Well, I can grab the one I'm reading from my bag."

Leo couldn't take his eyes off her. She wasn't dressed up, like yesterday. Today she wore a pair of dark jeans with tan ankle boots and a baggy, light beige T-shirt that said, "Twine Ball or Bust." Her eyes were lightly shadowed, and her lips had a hint of pink colour on them. She looked so wholesome, so confident.

"What? Do I have something on my face?" she said.

"No. I'm impressed with your suggestion. Why a book?"

"Not any book, a romance. It's a beach accessory almost every woman has in her bag."

"I'll use your book. It's a great idea."

"Thanks." Her cheeks flushed from his praise, something she was apparently lacking from the one person who mattered the most to her career.

As he waited for Karen to return with her romance novel, he moved props around and took some shots from different angles, all the while thinking back on what Natasha had said about Karen.

"What do you mean she doesn't belong here?" he'd asked her.

"She knows nothing of what fashion is today. I don't know if I can help her."

"It's your job to teach her. This industry is killer."

"Her background is in business. She should stay with what she knows."

"She apparently wants to be in New York's fashion world, Nat. Why can't you show her the ropes without being, well...a diva?"

Natasha had turned her attention back to the runway. "Perhaps. Fashion was not easy for me. It shouldn't be easy for her."

"Ah. So, you're teaching her all the hard lessons you had to endure."

"Yes."

"Shouldn't you be molding her, shaping her, preparing her for this double-edged world called fashion? Helping her fulfill her dreams.

"She believes we are equals."

"Did she say that?"

"Not exactly, but she cannot keep her mouth shut."

Leo had smiled. She'd never been able to.

"I cannot work with someone like that."

"You mean you won't."

Karen's muffled laugh interrupted his thoughts. She handed the book to him. "It's quite good and recommended on Goodreads."

A pocket-sized book with a generic cover. *Perfect.*

And he had a great idea. "While we wait for the model to get here, why don't you sit on the stool so I can take some sample shots and check lighting?"

"Umm...no, that's okay." Her eyes surveyed the room, searching for the model. "I don't do pictures."

"Come on. It'll be fun."

Karen's brows arched in question as she frowned.

"But more professional than fun. I really need to check the lighting...please?"

She nodded and stood in front of the beach back-drop. "Where do you want me?"

He let that question linger between them for a moment before answering. "Sit on the stool and put on the shades and hat."

After a few shots and poses, Leo noticed her loosening up. Even having some fun. Her smile lit up their corner. Her whole demeanour changed as she posed serious, then funny, then naughty. If he wasn't careful, he'd need to hide his crotch behind the wide-brimmed hat.

"Okay, on the towel with the book."

Karen lay on her belly, feet up and crossed at the ankles. She opened the book to her bookmarked page and read. The pose was so real and so in the moment that   Leo forgot to snap the shot. Instead, he watched her become so absorbed in what she was doing, it was like she was alone in her living room, relaxed and happy.

"Mr. St. Clare. So sorry I'm late. Stupid taxi got stuck in traffic."

Leo held up a hand to silence the model who'd arrived. "Are you ready to go, or do you still need makeup?"

"I'm ready," she squeaked.

"Good. Grab the hat and sunglasses and go stand in this corner." He turned back to Karen, but she was gone.

Chapter 3

As Karen made her way to each station checking on things, making sure everyone had their props, costumes and coffees, her gaze kept drifting to Leo in his tucked-away corner of the studio. He commanded such presence and respect from the models with whom he'd been assigned to work she hadn't had to go and fix anything. To her annoyance, this saddened her.

But why? Wasn't she mad at him? He'd entered her life again like nothing had happened between them. And she might have been able to deal with that and tell him to go where the sun doesn't shine. But no. She worked with him. Or for him? No. She would not work *for* him.. The man who had left without a word and humiliated her when she'd had to make the walk of shame from his dorm room and out the front door in front of all his friends—alone.

She remembered the catcalls and whistles and her skin being on fire from embarrassment. *Where had he gone? Why had he left her alone? Why had his friends thought it was funny to embarrass her? Had this been a common occurrence?* Had he brought so many women back to his dorm room that they were the butt of jokes? As the days had turned into weeks, with no contact from Leo at all, she'd felt used and dirty. Memories of her high-school bullying days had returned with a vengeance. Her newly found self-confidence had plummeted to an all-time low.

She'd never really know until she asked him. The real question was whether she wanted to know the answers to her questions. Was it worth any heartache she might revive? She wanted to believe he'd changed, but back then he'd done or said anything to get what he wanted. How was now any different?

Karen's cell phone buzzed in her back pocket. It was Natasha. With a sigh, she answered.

"Hello, Ms. Vale."

"How are things going over there?"

"Running smoothly."

"No disasters? All the material worked?"

"Well, the corsets aren't working. I made some alterations so the models can—"

"You made alterations without asking me first?"

Karen's heartbeat roared in her ears. "Well, we were tight on time and the models were complaining about not being able to—"

"I don't give a rat's ass about any of that. You get those corsets on those girls now and reshoot everything. Do you understand me?"

"Yes, ma'am," she said over the beep that told her she'd been hung up on. Natasha's anger echoed in her head as she gathered everyone and let them know their day had been extended for the reshoot. By way of an explanation, she sacrificed her feel-good day and took the blame.

Well, she had two ways to take care of this: be as grumpy as the models and crew, which would most likely drag out the reshoot, or make it fun—be anti-Natasha. She knew she wasn't the most senior person there, and therefore had no authority whatsoever, but her boss had told her to get it done, and that's what she was going to do. But she was going to do it her way. Damn the consequences.

Isn't that what keeps getting you in trouble? You don't think things through.

Clapping her hands, she got everyone's attention.

"Okay, people. I know it's late, but we need to re-shoot the nude suit. Ms. Vale has asked me to get this done, and I hope we can make it fun."

A few rumbles from the crowd didn't deter her. "Yes, fun. We'll turn it into a game. A competition. Instead of doing only one shoot and having everyone else stand around, let's break into groups and get every-one doing it." She spotted the two assistant photog-raphers gathered on one of the stages. "Pierre, Marc—take a model each and assemble a team. We have three corsets and nude swim suits. Change your backdrops and props. Be creative. Use your team. Get suggestions from everyone."

The rumbles turned into an excited buzz as people rushed around in different directions, gathering props and setting up new sets.

"Let's get this done fast—but right. Who can be done in two hours?"

People scurried, and soon team leaders emerged in each group as   models were squished back into the corsets.

"Ms. Allen?"

"Yes, Yvette?" She turned to the pretty redhead who had worn the corset earlier.

"I am not happy about this. I want to be able to breathe."

There had to be something she could do. A way for Natasha to see the ribbing of the corset under the nude suit while keeping the models from suffocating.

Taking the corset off the hanger, she examined the material closely. She pulled her cell phone out of her back pocket, searched the Internet for corset hacks, and hit the jackpot.

"Ms. Allen? Where are you going?"

"I need scissors." Karen took off, corset in hand, to find the seamstress. She wasn't at her station, which gave Karen the perfect opportunity to cut without being reamed out. Cutting two inches off the bottom of the corset gave leeway for breathing without interrupting the shape, which was more important than tightness—to a point. If this worked for Yvette, it would work for the other two models, who she could see out of the corner of her eye were still trying to get into the corsets.

"Yvette, here. Try this on."

"Ms. Vale will have your hide for this," Yvette said as she took the shortened material and disappeared behind the change curtain.

Fear took hold at that thought. Would Natasha really freak out if she made this corset issue work? Well, she had gotten upset about her other idea. She was stepping on her boss's toes—big time. But she'd make her understand, even if that meant more menial jobs. Hell, she'd even shine her shoes. That was how much the internship meant to her...and to Anna. She couldn't let her down. After all, it had been Anna and Jace who'd lit the spark under her low self-confidence and turned it into a flame of positive energy when she'd been hiding behind business school because she'd always thought herself less talented than Anna, who designed her own clothes.

Karen, though—she liked to fix the designs. Change and tweak them. Add to them. Put her mark on them. She'd even been fiddling with a design that, when she was famous, would be what she was recognized for. That thought made her smile.

»»·««

Her smile lit up the room and was contagious. Who knew she'd have such a commanding way about her? This was the old Karen that Leo remembered. The woman he'd met again recently was meek and timid. Eager to please. He hadn't liked it.

"Hey."

She turned to face him, her smile still big and bright. "Hey. How's it going over there?"

The power behind that smile warmed him to his toes.

"Well, we're still trying to get Gabby into the corset. The team is running out of ideas and getting disgruntled."

"Yvette. Did it work?"

Yvette stepped from behind the curtain and smiled. "Genius."

Karen did a happy dance and Leo laughed. It did look good.

"I cut two inches off the top."

Was she insane? "Karen—"

Karen shook her head. "I know, I know. I messed with another of Ms. Vale's ideas, but the corsets aren't her design. She bought them off eBay."

"That's not the point."

"The point is that I make this idea of hers work. What she doesn't know won't hurt her."

"Yes, I get that, but—"

"But what? Why should all these people suffer because she's a tyrant and likes to make everyone's life miserable? She makes mine miserable more times in a day than I can count. The least I can do is make it less hurtful."

"Or are you purposefully trying to make everyone hate her and make you out to be a hero?"

Karen stared back at him, her eyes big and her face an empty mask. "She's done a fine job of that all on her own." Her voice came out as a whisper, her anger barely in check.

As she took off across the room, Leo wanted to go after her, but instead he picked up his camera and headed back to where his team now had Gabby in her corset with the nude one-piece bathing suit over top. It was a unique idea, but not fully developed. Lace would have been a nice touch.

And what had he been thinking, berating Karen like that? When she was standing up to the woman who treated her like crap every day. Karen was flourishing in this environment—calling the shots, problem solving—and he had gone and stomped all over that with his words of discouragement. He had meant well. He didn't want her to get into trouble again.

His cell phone revved like a Mustang. It was his brother, Luke.

"Hey, Luke. What's going on?"

"Nice to hear from you too." Leo rolled his eyes and waited for him to continue. "Mom needs you to hit up a winery in the Hudson Valley. It's for sale, and she needs to know if it's a possible asset."

"In other words, she wants me to snoop around."

"Can't get anything past you."

Leo switched his phone to the other ear. "What about Dad?"

Luke let out a long sigh. "He doesn't want to cause any waves, so he's humouring her."

"Sounds normal." Their parents had an unorthodox relationship. During their marriage, bitterness and regret had filled their home, but once they'd divorced, they'd gotten along surprisingly well, and the winery business they'd started when Luke was born had blossomed into an international success. Leo had learned from that. As far as he was concerned, why suffer the heartache of marriage when you could be happy as friends with benefits? It had worked for him so far.

"Well, I'm busy doing a job right now. Why can't you go?"

Luke chuckled. "What job? We all know you're in New York for the eye candy."

"Who isn't? I got hired for my photography skills. I'm on set right now doing a shoot for an old friend, a side job during Fashion Week."

Dead silence on the other end. "Really?"

Oh, for goodness sake. Was he really the guy who played so hard even his own family didn't take him seriously? "Natasha Vale, head designer at Vale Designs. Look her up."

"And this photography job, is it consuming all of your time right now?"

Leo rubbed his throbbing temple. "I'm taking it day by day, but I'm going to say yes."

"Okay, I'll let Mom know you can't get away. She'll want to talk to you."

Yes, she will. "Why can't you go?"

"I'm in California right now overseeing things here while Mom and Dad are at their annual meetings in France."

Each of them in a different part of the world. He really was the only one who could do this. But he wanted nothing to do with the family business, and he never missed a chance to tell them.

"I'll talk to you later, big brother. Let me know how it goes."

"Don't work too hard." Luke got in the last jibe before hanging up.

Well, his life sure wasn't all play now. That had all changed when he'd arrived in New York two days earlier and pulled Karen out of harm's way.

She'd changed a lot, and he of all people appreciated what time did to a person. It could wring you out like a load of laundry, leaving you dizzy and unable to figure out which was the right way up. That was how the last ten years have been for him—ever since his sister Emily had died. A decade of pain and guilt. He almost couldn't remember how it felt to be happy, excited, in love.

Karen had tried to fill that void during their college years, but he'd run. Away from her innocent, prying questions. Away from her patience and kindness. He didn't deserve to be happy after what he'd done. He wore his guilty conscience like a cloak, even after all this time. If anything, it weighed more than ever before.

"Mr. St. Clare?" The young girl with the ponytail and glasses tapped him on the shoulder.

"Yes?"

"We're ready if you are."

"That was quick."

"It's a race. We want to win."

Leo nodded his agreement. Yes, he wanted to win too, and not only this reshoot. He wanted to win a chance to see Karen's smile again...a smile that felt like a ray of brilliant sunshine after a long, dark night.

"Where is Ms. Allen?" he asked as he changed his lens and motioned for his model to take a seat on the beach chair.

"She's with wardrobe. The third team had a bit of trouble with the corset cuts."

Guess he'd have to wait for that smile. "Let's do this."

His team cheered, and he went to work.

»»·««

Karen watched how smoothly Leo's team transitioned from one pose to the next. He barely spoke but used hand signals and nodded his head when he needed something moved or adjusted. He was a joy to watch, almost hypnotising.

A cheer from the opposite corner drew her attention away. She headed over to find the team cheering on the model as she tried some risqué poses. Karen shook her head and smiled. That's what happened when an all-male team worked with a female model.

"Behave," she warned, and moved on. The final team was wrapping up.

"Excellent job, you guys," she called out, then headed back to wardrobe. As she started to hang up some of the set pieces, her phone rang. It was Ms. Vale. Checking up on her, no doubt. She knew she should answer it, but she stared at her phone as the screen lit up with firework bursts of orange, yellow, and green, the screen saver she'd picked for her boss.

"You gonna answer that?"

Leo looked fabulous standing there like a sexy rock star with his camera around his neck. His dark brown hair was messy from a hard day's work, and his golden eyes glowed mischievously. She almost forgot about the ringing phone in her hand.

"What? Oh, no. It's not important." She quickly pressed the button to ignore the call. "Are you all done?"

"We are." Cheers went up around them. "And it sounds like everyone else is too."

"I knew we could do it."

"I did too."

Karen smiled and tucked her phone back in her pocket. "It was a good day."

Leo reached out and grabbed her hand. "You did an amazing job today."

Karen froze as liquid warmth traveled up her arm from his touch. "Thank you."

"Are we actually getting along?" Leo asked.

His smile made her weak in the knees. "I think we are."

"Hmm..."

"Ms. Allen. We did it in under two hours."

Karen turned from Leo reluctantly. "Yes, we did it," she said, and everyone cheered.

They cleaned up, and then Karen ordered pizza for the crew while the models nibbled on fruit and sipped sparkling water. Leo found them a spot on a bench to enjoy their meal.

"Here." He pulled two beers from behind his back and passed her one. "I confiscated these from one of the coolers."

Karen took the bottle he offered, twisted off the cap, and drank deep and long. The ice-cold beer went down like water and hit the spot.

"Thank you. I needed that."

They ate their pizza in silence. Karen watched how the others interacted and envied the easy comradeship.

"I watched you today."

Leo took a pull of his beer then placed it down beside him. "And?"

"You're good at taking pictures and leading a team. Really good."

"Thanks."

"Welcome."

Silence stretched between them again. "I watched you too."

"You did?" She wiped some sauce off her lips.

"You were in your element. You owned this assignment. I hope Natasha sees the good you've done today."

"Oh, she'll see it, but she won't acknowledge it."

"I don't think—"

"I know so. Been there, done that."

"Perhaps. But Natasha might see this as a stepping stone for you and she may loosen the reins a bit."

"I don't think so."

Leo took a bite of his pizza and chewed slowly. "You're so pessimistic. What happened to the positive attitude and vibe you instilled in the teams today?"

"I want to know that when I get to the office tomorrow morning, I'll still have a job."

"Everyone here will vouch for you."

"Maybe. But all the senior staff left as soon as I split the teams up. I'm quite sure they ran back to Ms. Vale and tattled on me. That's why she called me earlier, and I..."

Leo's eyebrows arched in surprise. "That's who you hung up on, isn't it? I knew something was up."

"I'm not sorry for what I did." She placed her unfinished pizza on the napkin and stood.

"For hanging up on your boss. Or—"

"No."

"Or the successful day?"

"Both."

"Good for you."

Karen faced him and let out a weary sigh. "You're being sarcastic, aren't you?"

He stood and took her hands. Her knees went wobbly, and her smile matched. She'd soon be putty in his hands if he didn't stop staring at her like he wanted to devour her whole.

"You should be proud of the work you did today. I know the shots are going to turn out great, and you've earned trust and respect from these people. They will want to work with you again."

Oh, how she hoped so. But even though she'd only been there for a few months, she'd seen—hell, she'd experienced first-hand—the backstabbing that took place in the fashion world to reach the top. And if the person at the top didn't want you to succeed...you didn't.

"I've got to get things packed up and into the closets. I've got another couple of hours of work ahead of me yet." Karen pulled her hands out of Leo's grasp and stepped back.

"Get the assistants to do it."

"They'll be helping."

"Is there anything I can do to help?"

Karen tilted her head and smiled. "Well, since you offered, an extra pair of hands is always needed to make the work go faster."

Let's see what he does with that. When he said nothing, her heart sank. Oh, right. Mr. Leo St. Clare didn't do anything as menial as cleaning up—in other words, all talk, no action. How disappointing. Karen walked away, a dull ache forming in the pit of her stomach.

»»•««

He was speechless. The way Karen stood with her head tilted to the side and a sheepish grin on her face, he was thrown back to the night they'd made love. They'd lain there for hours talking about all kinds of silly things. His heart had been hers if she'd wanted it. He'd never been so smitten with anyone. Love, no. That emotion hadn't belonged in his heart anymore, but she'd somehow cracked through the hard shell he'd surrounded himself with. And to be honest, was quite content to hide behind. He'd never wanted to stay and chat with a girl afterward. All of it had been quite new and weird, but he'd liked it. He'd liked her.

Then the questions had gotten a bit too personal...

"Karen, wait." He caught up to her and grabbed her elbow. "I'll help."

"Humph..."

"What can I do?"

They walked past wardrobe, and Karen stuck her arm out to stop him. "Fold clothes."

Leo took one glance at the lingerie lying on the table and sighed.

He wanted to kiss the smirk right off her face. Instead, he grabbed a pile of hangers from the rack and headed to the closest table to fold pairs of tiny panties. Humbled, he kept his head down until he was finished.

An hour later, Leo stood outside waving goodbye to the last crew member as they hopped in a cab.

"Thanks for staying to help."

Karen stood beside him, bundled up in a long down-filled coat and a gorgeous yellow infinity scarf covering her head.

"It was no problem. I had fun."

"We had a great team."

"It was all you." He couldn't tell if the blush on her cheeks was from the cold or his compliment.

"It was everyone—"

"Don't sell yourself short."

Karen exhaled a frustrated sigh. The cloud of air lasted only moments before disappearing into the cold.

"You don't take compliments well, do you?"

She wrapped her arms around herself for warmth. "That's a matter of opinion."

No argument there. "Are you afraid of success?"

Her head snapped up to face him. Her green eyes sparkled in the lamplight. She took his breath away. "Why would you suggest such a thing?"

He didn't know, and right then he didn't care. The overwhelming urge to kiss her senseless was so strong it took everything in him not to grab her arms and pull her into his embrace.

The crackling sound of tires driving on packed snow brought his attention back to the present. Robert had arrived with the limo to take him home. "Do you need a ride?" he asked Karen.

"No thank you."

Robert came around to open the door for Leo. He'd have to tell him again that wasn't necessary. "Are you sure? I don't mind."

"I'm sure. Again, thank you for all the help today."

"No problem."

Karen made to leave then turned back. "Did you have fun at the gala last night?"

Surprise hit him like a brick wall when he realised they hadn't talked about the party at all. "The food was good."

Karen's half-hearted smile caused an ache in his stomach. "Have a good night."

"Sir?" Robert stood with the door open.

Leo got inside the limo but continued to watch Karen until he couldn't see her anymore. His body was numb from the cold, and his fingers tingled from the sudden hit of warmth. She was the most stubborn woman he'd ever known, and it drove him crazy. She was her own worst enemy. If she wanted to freeze her butt off, then so be it. Yet, as the limo pulled away, he felt like the biggest jerk in New York.

Chapter 4

Karen loved this time of day. Six in the morning on a blustery day didn't beckon too many people out of bed easily. The office was quiet, not a soul in sight. She could do whatever she liked, and today she wanted two hours to pore over the photos from last year. As she walked down the long hallway, she turned on all the lights, flicked on the radio, and grabbed the photo book from behind Natasha's assistant's desk. One of her co-workers had a daylight lamp to help with mood disorders, and that was where she sat as she studied the previous year's designs.

Clutches, jumpsuits, ponchos, mixed prints, capes, overalls, bomber jackets, crop tops, and denim were the hottest trends of the year before. The one that caught her eye and kept her coming back for a second and third look was the tuxedo. The straight lines and slim design took masculine attire and feminized it beautifully. Single lapels with shimmer and open-collared shirts showcased dazzling necklaces. Three-inch heels and bejewelled clutches completed the look. One word summed up these creations: stunning.

There was something timeless about the tuxedo—whether on a man or a woman, it never went out of style. Karen sensed the beginnings of her excitement when the butterflies in her stomach started to flutter non-stop and she couldn't sit still. Rummaging through her co-worker's desk, she found a pad of paper and a pencil and set to sketching what her brain had conjured so clearly.

The ding of the elevator bell startled her from her concentration. *Dammit.* She didn't want anyone to see her there. She tore off the piece of paper she'd been sketching on and stuffed it in her pocket. She tucked the pad and pencil back in the drawer and then turned off the lamp, grabbed the photo book, and made her way to the back of the room where the kitchen was located. The office was coming alive with voices. There was no way she was going to get the photo book back to its proper place without anyone seeing her.

"Karen?"

Pulse roaring in her ears, Karen turned around to find Stacey looking at her. *Shit.*

"You scared me to death. What is it?"

"Ms. Vale is looking for you."

"Okay, thanks. I'd better go. Don't want to keep her waiting, right?" Her gaze darted from Stacey to the door and back. Sweat formed on her upper lip as she tucked the photo book under her arm. She almost escaped out the door when she felt a tap on her shoulder.

"What is that?" Stacey nudged her chin at the book. "Looks like last year's photo book."

"This?" Karen mocked surprise as she held the album close to her chest.

Stacey pried the photo book from Karen's tight grasp and yanked it away. "This is last year's photo book," she squealed. "Why do you have it?"

"Well, I...you see..."

"You stole it from my bookcase." Her pointed finger was only an inch from Karen's nose. "My area is off-limits. How dare you."

"I didn't know it was off-limits. Stacey, wait."

Stacey took off at a run down the hall and made a beeline for Ms. Vale's office. Tackling Stacey to the ground made a delightful image, but an image was all it could be—when she burst into Ms. Vale's office without knocking, Karen knew she'd get punished.

As will I, she noted as she followed Stacey in.

"Stacey. What is the meaning of this?"

Stacey stammered as Ms. Vale marched up to her. Karen came to a grinding halt when she noticed Leo standing at the desk with photos in his hands. Their eyes met, and a zap of anxiety rushed down to her toes. Was he already showing the boss photos from yesterday's shoot? For some reason, she had thought they'd show Ms. Vale together, instead of her being beckoned by the assistant.

"Ms. Vale, Karen stole last year's photo book from my bookshelf, and I know you told me no one can touch anything on those shelves unless they ask you, so I came to tell you right away. I'm sorry for interrupting. Can I get you a coffee?"

Karen watched in awe as Stacey, without taking a breath during her verbal rampage, waved her arms like a magician about to do the world's best trick.

Ms. Vale turned her full attention on Karen now. "Is this true?" Her voice was barely above a whisper, and Karen had to strain to hear.

"I didn't know that shelf was off-limits."

Ms. Vale walked back to her desk and picked up the photos Leo had put down. "All the rules were outlined for you the day you were hired."

Karen sighed in frustration. "I'm sure they were, but—"

"You are expected to obey all the rules here at Vale Designs as everyone else does. I do not tolerate my rules being broken." She flipped through the pictures at lightning speed, which snapped the last bit of patience Karen had left.

"How are you seeing anything when you go that fast?" Karen blurted out. Stacey gasped then covered her mouth. Leo gave her a weary glance and shook his head as if telling her she was in for it now.

Ms. Vale tossed the photos down with such force they flew across the desk and landed on the floor.

"Now you're telling me how to do my job?"

"No. I asked a question—"

Ms. Vale launched into her once-a-week passionate speech about her career, how she'd had to scrape and claw to get where she was, and rules were in place for a reason. Karen tuned out and kept her attention focused on Leo. He really was a piece of work, standing there not caring about what was going on. It was obvious how much he valued his weeklong job over their friendship. Was she the only one who was paying attention to the spark that ignited when they were alone? Maybe she was repeating the past in thinking there was more between them than there actually was.

"Earth to Kara. Did you hear a word I said?"

"It's Karen."

Well, at least that hadn't come from her mouth this time. Karen looked at Leo and then Ms. Vale, who stopped her rant. *Look out, Leo, she's about to chop your head off.*

"Yes, of course. Really, you should think about changing your name. It's so plain I can never remember it."

Knife plunge in the chest and twist. Ouch.

"Ms. Vale?"

"What is it, Stacey?"

Stacey picked up a piece of paper off the floor and handed it to Ms. Vale. It was Karen's sketch. *It must have fallen out of my pocket.*

Natasha examined the wrinkled piece of paper for a long time. When her gaze finally left the paper and met Karen's, it was full of loathing.

"Is this yours?"

She knew if she were smart, she'd deny it.

"Yes."

"Is this your idea of a joke?" Natasha folded the paper carefully and tossed it onto her desk.

"Excuse me?" Karen's stomach was in knots and nausea rose up her throat. Ms. Vale was going to take her sketch. She wrung her hands to keep from reaching out and snatching the piece of paper off the desk.

"You sketched a copy of a design from last year? What were you hoping to achieve? You are so out of touch, it's laughable."

Heat flooded Karen's cheeks and spread to her neck. Was this happening in front of her ex-lover and the gossipiest woman she'd ever met?

"I knew you were washed up from the moment I met you."

Karen saw red. "How dare you?" she spat, and she charged at Natasha.

Leo stepped between them and put his hands on her shoulders. "Karen."

She looked into his eyes and saw concern, and maybe a lingering fear. For her or him, she couldn't tell. Her eyes grew large and wet, her tell-tale sign of a big cry, and Leo knew it. He spun her around and walked her to the door.

"Karen is going to get you a coffee," he called out, and he closed the door behind them.

Dammit. Dammit. Karen's mind screamed as Leo escorted her to the washroom. "What are you doing?" her voice squeaked in surprise as he followed her inside.

"You know the drill." His voice rumbled low and sexy, and her heart skipped a beat.

"Anyone in here?" she called out as she opened the three stall doors. Empty. "Coast is clear."

"Good."

Karen faced the mirror and gasped. Her face was as white as a sheet, her hair looked washed out, and her eyes looked too big for her face. *Zombie, anyone?*

"You okay?" She watched in the mirror as Leo approached her from behind. Standing like that together brought up past moments of wishful thinking about a happily-ever-after. The kind you had after a night of passionate lovemaking—*sorry, sex,* she reminded herself. No one left after *lovemaking* and never talked to you again. She shook her head to rid herself of those negative and unwanted thoughts. She had enough on her plate already without rehashing the past.

"Can you believe what she did in there? What she said?"

Leo met her gaze in the mirror, and then turned her around to face him. "Yes, I can believe it. And so can you."

"I—"

"After three months, you should've figured out how Natasha works."

"Well, yes, but—"

"She is a nasty little witch."

"Leo," she chastised, and she checked to make sure no one had walked in on them.

"And she has an ego as big as the city she lives in." Karen couldn't help but giggle. "But she's one of the best because of it."

"Whose side are you on?" she asked.

Leo stepped back and ran his hands through his hair, making it messy. No matter what he did, he always turned out gorgeous. Karen gave her head a shake.

"I'm here to do a job. One week and that's it. Then I'm outta here."

"Right." The deep hollowness in her stomach grew as she realised how artificial the connection between them these last couple of days had been. "Speaking of jobs, how did you get this one? I have a hard time picturing you sitting down to create a resumé and taking the time to apply for a job across the pond in the middle of winter when you could be sunbathing by your pool in Tuscany."

"I do have other talents besides sunbathing."

"Glad to hear it."

"Natasha called me."

They had been lovers, she realised. Probably were still. Why else would Natasha have his number? And when had this hollowness spread to her heart?

"You hang in the same circles then." Her voice hitched with emotion. Why did she even care? A few more days and he'd be gone.

"Used to—a long time ago."

She knew it. *Wait...* "What?"

"We were friends in high school senior year, but when my parents divorced, we moved away. Kept in touch but didn't really hang out anymore unless she had something to celebrate or launch."

Old friends? She wanted to believe him. "And your photography?"

"Passion of mine forever. It's more of a hobby than a career. Nat wanted amateur eyes not used to the fashion scene. She wanted a fresh perspective on this year's lines."

"Smart." Karen didn't know what else to say. Her sadness dissipated like steam off water.

"She is that."

"Why didn't you tell me any of this before?"

"You didn't ask."

Karen closed her eyes and took three deep breaths. Didn't help.

"You're still an insensitive, shallow jerk who thinks only of himself."

"Karen—"

"Here I thought I had a friend, an ally to make this internship more tolerable."

"You do."

"I don't. I'm alone...as always." She pushed him aside and walked out of the bathroom and to the elevator. It wasn't until the elevator doors closed that she succumbed to the anger building up inside her and punched the wall.

>>>·<<<

Leo had barely stepped inside his penthouse when his cell phone rang. He put the phone to his ear.

"You didn't have to call and check on me, Mom." She was waking up, and he was getting ready for bed. *Love that time difference.*

"Hi to you too."

First his brother and now his mom. He had to make more of an effort to say hello first when he answered their calls.

"Hi, Mom. How are you today?"

"Fine, darling. You?" His exhausted sigh apparently put his mom on high alert. "You are partying too much with those models and not getting enough sleep and exercise."

"I've been to one party since I've been here, and I'm in the weight room and pool every day." Sleep had been lacking, but she didn't need to know that. His mind refused to stop thinking about Karen. Even in his dreams he saw her naked body writhing beneath him that night in his dorm room. She'd been such a good friend to him in the short time he'd known her, it had made the act of sex with her mean something.

"You've talked to Luke?"

"Yeah. He mentioned you wanted me to check out a winery outside of town?"

"It would be lovely if you could. Since you're already there."

"Can you give me more details? Like location."

"It's an adorable little cottage about two hours north of the city. It's small but quite popular. The owners are looking to retire."

"Almost sounds too good to be true."

"Your father said the same thing. That's why I want you to go in person and see."

"I know nothing about wineries, Mom. I've purposely avoided learning anything about them."

His mother laughed, and it sounded so good. He missed her.

"Wineries are in your blood, Leopold. There is no escaping it. You've breathed and absorbed their essence right from birth."

"That's not possible, Mom."

"Anything is possible if you want it bad enough."

"I don't want—"

"Don't want it for yourself then. Want it for me."

The silence that followed didn't feel awkward or pressured like it often had in the past. He could do this for her. He was so close anyway, and Luke and his dad had other commitments.

"Okay. I'll do it."

"Are you sure? If you can't, I understand. You are a busy man."

"Mom, I said I'd do it."

"Thank you, darling. I'll send you an email with all the specs."

"Okay."

"Love you."

"Love you too, Mom."

The call ended, and he placed his phone on the table with his wallet. He was doing a good thing. He didn't have to commit past this one favour. He'd be able to return to his drag racing, parties, and women. It was what he wanted. It was what he was good at.

He made his way to the floor-to-ceiling windows that boasted a spectacular view of Times Square. No traffic or pedestrian sounds could bother him up here.

The streetlights below glittered like stars, but he didn't even notice, his mind on his mother's tone. She'd placated him. They all did. Luke not so much, but he still recognized it for what it was. His family didn't take him seriously, and it didn't bother him in the least. Or it hadn't until now.

Emily's death had changed the family. It separated his parents, and Luke had to grow up fast to help run the family business. As for Leo, he'd run. His need for adrenaline had gone from a hobby to a passion. He'd do anything he could to feel alive, to have the exhilaration of his heart pumping so fast he might burst. To simply feel and fill the void in his centre that had belonged to his sister.

Karen had tried, although unknowingly, to fill that void with her care and concern all those years ago. And he'd panicked and run again. Would he ever stop running?

He looked out at the lights below him. Boring. He'd seen it all. That initial euphoria of seeing and doing something new was gone. He hadn't realised how much he missed that feeling.

A flashing red heart on one of the billboards caught his eye. Valentine's Day. He'd forgotten about the commercialized day of love for some and bitterness for most. Well, he didn't have any plans. Tomorrow he'd order flowers for the office. An extra-large bouquet for Natasha—she'd expect nothing less.

And Karen. The thought of wining and dining her appealed to him more than taking this photography gig. Leo moved away from the window. Yes, he liked that idea. A lot.

He dialled the number of one of his favourite restaurants and made a reservation. Leo couldn't wait to ask her.

»»·««

"You did not."

"Come on, Karen. He's a great guy."

Karen had agreed to meet her roommate, Mike, for lunch at their favourite little café overlooking Central Park. Over bowls of mushroom soup and fresh French bread, he'd spilled the beans. She'd been set up on a blind double date for Valentine's Day.

She scooped some soup onto her spoon and blew on it before sipping. "I know you don't remember much about our high school days, Mike, but I've never been a fan of Valentine's Day."

"Oh, I remember," he started as he pulled a chunk of bread off the loaf and dipped it in his soup. "Especially since I was the unlucky bloke who had the nerve to ask you in grade eleven."

Karen's head tilted back with her laugh. "Ah, yes. Poor Mike."

The café was full of people squished around tiny tables. The hum of conversation was loud, so to hear anything from the person sitting across from you required raising your voice. The smell of freshly baked bread, rosemary, and coffee beans filled the air, and the waitress kept up with the chaos with good spirits. This was not a place to come for peace and quiet. This was where Karen liked to come to get energized and lost in a New York experience.

"The four of us will meet at the house after work tomorrow."

"The four of us?"

Mike took another sip of his soup before answering. "Paul has set me up with a blind date as well."

"Whaaatt?" Karen laughed, unable to believe what she'd just heard.

"I don't want to talk about it," he mumbled.

"Okay, fine. Can I at least ask where we're going?

"That is mine and Paul's surprise for you ladies."

"Paul? Do I know him?"

"He's a colleague of mine."

Karen's eyes narrowed as she sat back in her chair. "Is he going to be a boring stiff then?"

Mike choked down the soup in his mouth. "What?"

"I mean, you're an exception to the rule, but most lawyers—"

"Stop worrying. I hang out with Paul all the time. He's fun." He wiped his mouth with his napkin. "You'll like him."

"Fine."

They ate the rest of their food in silence. Why did the idea of a double date upset her? Mike would never set her up with some jerk he didn't know. There would be four of them, so if things didn't work out, there would be a safety net.

If she were honest with herself, she couldn't get Leo out of her head. That morning half a dozen bouquets had come to the office and were placed on random desks, none on hers. Natasha's bouquet was stunning, with blood red roses and red lilies interspersed with baby's breath. Everyone knew who the flowers had come from. Karen knew it was a grand gesture to make sure no one felt left out, and she appreciated that.

Yet for some reason she took offence that nothing special had been on her desk. Each day the obvious hints were dropped in front of her that she didn't mean anything to him anymore. She'd have to figure out how to be okay with that, and step one was to accept this date and move on.

"It'll be more than fine, Mike. Tell Paul I'm looking forward to meeting him."

"Excellent." A mixed look of surprise and happiness on his face had Karen laughing again.

"And I'll be good, I promise."

"That's what I was worried about." He sighed in relief as he tossed down some cash to pay for the meal.

»»•««

Karen placed her coat on the back of her desk chair and took a sip of her latte. The energy that hummed through the office was contagious, and she couldn't help but smile. Sunshine peaked through the slits in the blinds and cast rainbows on the walls from the prism that hung in the centre window. Someone had taken all the flowers and put them in the foyer near the elevator. The floral scent overwhelmed the small space, but visually it was gorgeous.

"Hey, you busy?"

Leo sat on the corner of her desk. His grey shirt stretched across his shoulders and tapered down to his waist. Karen's fingers itched to trace his abs. He should not have been allowed to dress like that at work. She refused to let her gaze linger too long on his legs in those jeans.

"I...uh...no. Got back from lunch a few minutes ago. What's up?" *Good save.* She gave herself a mental high-five, even though her cheeks burned with embarrassment at having been caught checking him out.

"I want to go over those corset prints with you."

Taken aback, Karen held onto her coffee cup with shaking hands. "Why?" Her question came out harsher than she'd wished. "I mean, why with me? Isn't that something you and Natasha have to do?"

"I haven't had a chance to show her these ones yet. I thought you and I could grab some coffee and take a look."

"Already have the coffee." She lifted her cup up to show him. "Let's go into the kitchen and I'll make you a cup."

Leo turned up his nose. "Office coffee? Are you serious?"

"You're right. I don't know what I was thinking," she said, hiding her smirk behind her coffee cup.

"Can you get away?" His golden eyes held her in place and time slowed down. He covered her hand with his. His hands were a mixture of rough calluses and smoothness, and oh, they were so warm.

"I'd love to—"

"Karen. Ms. Vale wants these prints filed in the next hour, and then she wants you to go and get her dry cleaning." Stacey dropped a huge pile on her desk before sauntering away.

"But I can't," Karen finished, and she sat back in her chair with a weary sigh.

Leo's cell phone beeped an incoming text. "It's Nat," he said as he read it. "I have another shoot tonight. Wanna come along? I could use your insight."

Karen's heart raced with excitement. Another chance to put her touch on designs being used in the Fashion Week shows made her giddy.

"What is it this time?"

"Fur coats."

"Hmm…" Luxurious furs. Not much to be done there. But it would be more time with Leo. After her big freak-out episode in the washroom earlier, she'd realised she needed to be in his good books. He'd stuck up for her in Natasha's office. She could imagine how helpful he'd be if they weren't at each other's throats all the time.

"Okay, I'm in. Where is it?"

His fingers flew across the screen of his phone. "The Rockefeller Center ice rink."

"Wow. Haven't been there yet."

Leo looked up from his phone. "Seriously?"

"I'm afraid so." Karen started to sort through the pile on her desk.

"Well, then this will be quite the adventure."

"There won't be any adventure for me if I don't get this done."

"Right." Silence stretched between them, clarifying the mundane sounds of a photocopier and a phone ringing nearby.

"What time shall I meet you?" Karen asked as she grabbed her latte and took a small sip.

"Six. I can pick you up at your place."

"I'll still be here."

Leo ran a hand through his hair. "Okay. Six o'clock out front?"

"It's a date."

Leo smiled and sat his cute little behind back on the corner of her desk. "A date?"

"Well…it's a figure of speech."

"Is it?"

"It is," she said and waved her hand, causing a few prints to fly off the pile and onto the floor. "Dammit."

Leo and Karen hunched down at the same time, knees touching and their faces only a breath apart. "I can get them," she said, her breath shallow and wispy.

"So can I." His eyes darkened to the colour of molten honey as his gaze dropped to her lips. She licked them and he growled. The sound excited her, and she started to tremble.

"Leo, I…"

He exhaled slowly and closed his eyes, and the connection was lost. Standing, he extended his hand and helped her up. "Here you go." He handed her the prints and stepped back. "See you at six?"

Karen nodded and watched him leave. Sitting back down, she willed her pulse to its normal rhythm. How had that happened? That was not what she'd had in mind when she'd told herself to get in his good books. They'd *almost* kissed. At work. In front of a bunch of gossiping busy bodies. That couldn't happen again.

She tackled the pile of prints with a vengeance and spent the next hour alphabetizing and going back and forth to Stacey's desk asking for each binder as she needed them. Stacey wouldn't let anything off her shelves or out of her line of sight. By the time she'd made the cold trek to the dry cleaners, Karen's body ached, and she had to fight to keep her eyes from drooping closed.

The store was busy. People were dropping off and picking up garments, and some were chatting near the window, prolonging the inevitable—having to go back outside. As she waited for her turn, an incredible exhaustion took over and her nose started to drip. Digging in her purse for a tissue, she didn't see the two women who walked in.

"If it ain't Miss Goody Two Shoes."

Karen looked up and saw two women she worked with who were Stacey's BFFs and rented out the space around the water cooler. For the life of her, she couldn't remember their names. She'd improvise.

"Well, if it ain't Barbie One and Barbie Two." She noticed their scowls and blew her nose.

"What are you doing here?" Barbie One asked as she ran her hand up and down her mink stole.

"My job."

"Yeah, well, you took Stacey's job, and she's miserable." Barbie Two clicked the gum she chewed then blew a big bubble.

"I'm the intern. I do all the menial tasks for everyone, including Stacey, as per Ms. Vale's strict instructions. Right now, I am here to pick up her dress."

Barbie One sauntered up to Karen so they were only inches apart. "Look, you might know and say all the right things, but you will never fit in." Her gaze dragged over Karen's body slowly, and through the layers her skin burned and sweat kicked in.

"And wavy hair is sooo last year," Barbie Two chimed in. "What's with the highlights anyway? Makes your hair look dirty."

"Why do you insist on wearing clothes that hang on you? We know you have no figure, but really," Barbie One added.

"Enough." Richard rushed from behind the counter and stood beside Karen, his hands gesturing wildly. All of this seemed to be happening from miles away, and because she was sweating, her body cooled rapidly and shivering kicked in. Her heartbeat roared in her ears...and she was twelve years old again, but not alone. This time she had a friend.

"You will apologise to Ms. Allen, and then you will leave my store and never come back. If I so much as see you walk by my window, I will put in a personal call to Ms. Vale and have you both fired faster than you can say 'tacky.'"

Karen would've laughed at their feeble attempts at an apology, but she was in awe of Richard and what he'd done for her.

"Thank you so much." Her voice was shaky, and her tired eyes started to burn.

"You are welcome, darling. I hope this does not cause any issues for you at work." Even if it did, Karen knew she'd be okay. One word from her to Richard, and the Barbie twins would be out of a job. She swiped at a tear that rolled down her cheek. Her first bully protector was a world-famous tailor to the stars and her first New York friend.

Chapter 5

Leo picked Karen up at six o'clock sharp from work. She thanked Robert as he held the door open for her and she slipped inside the cozy limo. She sank into the seat with a sigh, savouring the bliss of being off her feet.

"Rough afternoon?"

Karen turned to look at Leo through her droopy eyelids. "You could say that."

She watched as his gaze roamed her face. "You do look a bit pale. Are you sure you want to come along? I can get Robert to drop you off at home."

Karen closed her eyes and turned her head back. "You won't give up on the driving-me-home angle, will you?"

Leo huffed and passed her some prints. "I can find where you live easily enough. Now go through these and tell me what you think."

He was smooth. Karen sat up straight and cleared her throat. She focused on the first image and gasped. It wasn't a picture of the gorgeous model in the teeny-tiny corset; it was a picture of her lying on a beach towel reading.

"I don't understand." Her voice came out as a whisper.

"Tell me what you see."

She saw a scrawny, unfashionable girl pretending to be a model.

"Try again."

Karen bit her lower lip and chanced a glance at Leo. His eyes flared, and his mouth was set in a deep frown. She'd spoken her thoughts out loud again.

"Umm...I see a girl reading a book..."

Leo grabbed the prints out of her hand and tossed them on the seat across from them. "Are you purposely being obtuse?"

Karen inhaled sharply. "No—"

Leo took hold of her wrists and urged her toward him, so she was pretty much sitting on his lap. "I don't know this girl you speak of. The girl I know is funny and witty and doesn't take crap from anyone."

"That may be the girl you knew."

"What happened to her? To you? I see glimpses of the old you when you fight with Natasha, but then—"

"But then it takes a lot for me to keep pretending to be strong, and unfortunately you've seen me at my worst. I'm pathetic."

"Never, but different from my memories."

Karen slid off his lap and moved to the seat where he'd tossed the prints. "Maybe I was never like that, Leo."

"I don't believe it."

She passed the prints back to him. "What do you see?"

He scanned the picture on top for a long time then handed it back to her. "I see a young, beautiful woman full of love and dreams. I see how enthralled you are in that book even with all the chaos going on around you. You're relaxed and carefree as if you really were on a tropical holiday. But I also see confidence in your pose and a little bit of fun in the way you have your ankles crossed and the tip of the beach hat."

Karen's gaze strayed to the image he'd created in words. It sounded fabulous...and fake. "You didn't show these to Ms. Vale, did you?"

Leo sighed and leaned back in his seat. "No."

"Good." She nodded her head once in confirmation.

"She's seen the other prints."

Karen held her breath. Why was he being so mysterious? "And?"

He sat forward, his focus on her. "And she didn't even notice the adjustments."

She wanted to jump for joy. She'd known it would work. "Did she like them?"

"Very much," he said.

"Okay, Mister Grumpy Pants. Why does it sound like you aren't happy about that? We stayed overtime to get this done right."

"She took full credit for it."

Ouch. "That sounds like Natasha Vale."

"Doesn't it bother you at all?" He crossed the small space and turned to face her. Their knees touched, and a jolt of awareness ran up her leg. Long limo rides were not a good idea with this man, as the close confinement played havoc with her sanity.

"A...a...bit," she stammered. She made the mistake of looking him in the eye and gasped. He looked like he wanted to devour her.

"And?"

"And...if this little costume save keeps her from flipping her lid and firing me, then the secrecy is worth it."

The lust in his eyes disappeared. "That's ridiculous."

"Losing my job is not ridiculous." Anger burned in her chest. "You never have to worry about self-preservation. You always got what you wanted, and you still do. You will always be the Golden Lion."

Her cheeks burned as she stared out the window. She spotted the Rockefeller Plaza street sign and knew they were close. She gathered her purse close to her side and placed her hand on the door handle.

"Karen, please. You misunderstood me—"

"No, I didn't."

The limo stopped. She didn't wait for Robert to open the door for her. The cold air was refreshing after being cooped up in the limo. People moved past her at a brisk pace and jazz music boomed out for all to hear. Couples and young kids skated around the ice rink. Laughter rang out, and the aroma of coffee and hot dogs from nearby vendors filled her nostrils. This area of midtown Manhattan emitted a happy vibe Karen couldn't help but notice.

"The crew is set up in the far corner." Leo stood behind her, his hand on the small of her back, and the warmth radiated through her jacket. The feeling soothed her.

He guided her through the crowd to a secluded spot near the water fountain. A canopy was set up, with chairs for the models getting hair and makeup done. Space heaters were situated in each corner, and a coffee station near the back called out her name. With a cup in hand, Karen made her rounds. She had to admit the teams she'd worked with this week were a dream compared to the usual high-maintenance ones she normally got assigned.

The fur-themed photo shoot featured ankle-length and mid-thigh coats with bikinis underneath. A pale mint backdrop draped in green shamrock balloons, emerald streamers, and lots of faux diamonds was situated in front of the fountain. Green tinted water completed the St. Patrick's Day theme.

"This is quite the set-up." Karen picked up a diamond necklace and admired the rainbow shimmer as she turned it side to side.

"Cubic zirconia," Leo commented as he stood beside her adjusting his camera lens.

"Are the furs real?"

"No way. Too controversial."

A glam shoot without the expense. The first model arrived, and Karen helped pose her and adjust props, and then she stood near the back and watched Leo work. He put the model, Sarah, at ease with some jokes and then began. His movements were fluid, his tone polite, and his skill superb. He changed the camera lenses with the blink of an eye. The lighting crew knew his hand signals, and within the hour Sarah's session was done.

"Next," Leo called out.

When no one came out, Karen searched for the next model. "What's going on? Mr. St. Clare is waiting."

The makeup artist shrugged. "Kim said she was nauseous and ran off in search of the bathroom."

"Hmm…okay. Who's after her?"

"Sarah again. We only have the two models for this shoot."

"We'll need a bit of time to get Sarah ready. I'll go get her."

Leo looked up when Karen emerged from the tent. "Is something wrong?"

"Kim's not feeling well. She's in the washroom." Karen nodded her head at Sarah. "We need you back in the makeup chair to get ready for the next shoot. Hopefully Kim will be back by the time you're done."

"Yes, Ms. Allen."

Karen avoided looking at Leo until she could feel his gaze on her. "What?"

"You're in your element at these shoots."

The burning in her cheeks radiated to the roots of her hair. "What do you mean?"

Leo stood and placed his camera on the table beside him. His stare penetrated right to her soul, exposing vulnerabilities she'd buried deep. "Stop it," she said.

"You are amazing." His golden eyes lit up as his gaze dropped to her lips.

"Don't."

"You are talented." His voice grew huskier with each word.

"Please...don't..."

"And so beautiful." His lips were only inches from hers now.

"No—"

"Ms. Allen?"

Karen jumped back. With her pulse in overdrive and her vision blurred, she turned around. "Yes?"

"Kim's back, but I don't think she's doing too well."

Karen collected her thoughts and got her bearings, but her pulse still raced. "Thanks, Sarah. I'll speak to her. Are you ready for Mr. St. Clare?"

"Yes."

Karen didn't look back at Leo before entering the tent. Kim was sitting in a corner with her arms wrapped around her middle and a bucket at her feet.

"Hey, Kim. How are you feeling?"

The young girl looked up at her. She couldn't be younger than eighteen, but with the gaunt cheekbones and desperate look in her eyes, she looked more like twelve.

"Not good." Her voice was hoarse.

"You've been throwing up?"

"Yeah."

"Why don't you tell me what's going on?" Karen hoped it was only the stomach flu, but she didn't think so.

"I'm late."

A stab of pity hit her hard in the stomach. "Are you sure?"

Kim nodded then grabbed the bucket. After a few dry heaves, Karen passed her a tissue.

"What do you want to do?"

"I can't keep it. I'll lose my job, and I'll never be able to model again." Her eyes radiated pure desperation. Karen couldn't fathom having to choose between a baby and a job. But in Kim's case, she probably didn't have any schooling past high school and had been living off her beauty—whatever that brought her. In this case, an unwanted baby.

"Please don't tell Ms. Vale. I'll be ruined." Tears flooded her eyes, and her sigh hitched with her silent sobs.

Karen dug through her purse and found some ginger melts that she always keeps on hand due to too many digestive upsets eating on the run since starting this job. "Here. Take this. Hopefully you can keep it down."

Kim popped the melt into her mouth and once it dissolved, she chased it down with the little bit of water from her bottle. "Thanks," she said.

"You're welcome, and I won't tell Ms. Vale, but you'll need to decide what you're going to do soon. You know how gossip spreads in this industry."

"But if I deal with it on my own first, maybe take a few days off, you could cover for me—"

"I won't lie to Ms. Vale, Kim. You're asking me to put my job on the line."

"We were told not to get knocked up or we'd be out on our ass."

Karen believed that. "What happened? If this career means so much to you, why did you let this happen?"

Kim leaned back in her chair and exhaled slowly. "Have you ever fallen for a sweet-talker who promised you the moon? Well, he promised that and more, until he got me between the sheets. I haven't heard from him since... It's been six weeks."

Karen's body went numb. Yes, she'd fallen for that type of guy once. Fortunately, a baby hadn't followed.

"Do you love him?"

Kim bent forward and reached for the bucket. "Thought I did. Thought we'd get married too. I am so stupid."

Karen rubbed Kim's back. "Not stupid. Naïve, yes. How long were you seeing each other?"

"A week."

Karen gasped but didn't stop rubbing Kim's back. "Well, okay...maybe a bit stupid."

Kim laughed, long and hard.

"Hey, you guys okay in here?" Leo walked in, followed by Sarah.

"We're good. You?"

"We did great. Sarah is a pro. You ready for a turn at this merry-go-round, Kim?"

"I need five minutes in the makeup chair."

"Take ten. I need a quick break."

Karen helped Kim stand and escorted her to the chair. "I want her vulnerability to pop. Don't add any colour to her cheeks. Make her eyes bigger. Have her bangs partially covering the right side of her face."

The makeup artist nodded and got right to work.

"Ms. Allen?" Kim said.

"Yes?"

"Thank you."

"You're welcome. And don't worry, we'll figure this out."

Kim's smile eased a bit of the anxiety that had started to grow in Karen's belly. She sought out Leo and found him at the coffee station. Would he help, or had he done his good deed for the week when he'd stood up for her earlier?

Joining him at the table, Karen topped off her coffee. "So, she's pregnant, hey?"

Karen's eyebrows shot up in surprise. "Umm..."

"Swore you to secrecy?"

"Well, no..."

"No, she's not pregnant or no to secrecy?"

Oh, he was maddening. *How on earth did he know? Was he the baby daddy? No, that was ridiculous.* She shook her head a few times and changed her train of thought. No good would come from that tangent. She needed his help, not these dark thoughts.

"Well, she might be. But there could be a ton of other reasons why she's throwing up."

"For her sake, I hope it's a ton of other reasons."

There was no point arguing with him. Karen hoped so as well.

"In the meantime, we need to keep this from Ms. Vale."

Leo took a sip of his coffee then placed the cup on the table, his gaze never leaving her face. "You want me to lie to the boss?"

"Not a bold, flat-out lie. Spin a tall tale when asked. Or play dumb for all I care."

"You're going to put your internship on the line for a teenage model who's made some bad decisions?"

Karen frowned and stepped back. "I'm not agreeing with her choices, and trust me, she's made some pretty dumb ones that I can relate with, but I am not going to stand by and watch her be bullied by my boss, which is what will happen whether she's pregnant or not. I don't need your help. You do whatever helps you sleep better at night, and I'll protect this young girl as much as I can, while I can." Karen's rant ended as abruptly as it had started. Her cheeks were on fire and her breath short and laboured. Leo stood there with a bored expression on his face and his coffee cup back in his hand. He really didn't care, it seemed, and the ache below her heart expanded to her stomach. She'd never felt so alone.

Any steam left from her passionate speech evaporated, leaving her bone tired. The fight was gone. It was a tough one to keep playing alone. "I'm not feeling well, either," she blurted out. "I'll see you tomorrow."

Leo grabbed her arm. "You can't leave. I need you— your help with Kim."

Karen shook her head and shrugged her arm from his grasp. "You don't need me. Kim will be fine. She may be young, but she's a professional."

Turning, she walked out of the tent and into the brisk night. The faux diamonds shimmered in the streetlight, creating a magical world Leo would no doubt capture and bring to life. She envied his natural talent and his self-confidence. His nonchalant attitude awarded him a stress-free life. Living in Tuscany and lounging around the pool all day probably helped a lot, too. Hailing a cab, she went home. Thoughts of a hot bath to ward off the chill warmed her during the quick ride.

»»·««

He had to admit she looked beautiful. The camera loved Kim's vulnerability. The sadness in her eyes spoke to him, made him want to solve all her problems for her.

Karen was right. And it bummed him out that she wasn't there to see yet again one of her ideas bloom into brilliance. If only he could make her see how talented she was—make her believe it. She'd be unstoppable.

But he was only in New York until the end of the week. He didn't have the time to break Karen Allen out of her shell. He did, however, have time to take her out for Valentine's night.

Thinking about the dinner reservations he'd made and the dozen red roses that were on order to be picked up on the way to her house excited him. Until he remembered how she'd stormed out of there. She'd been hurt by what he'd said, and he'd been a callous dumbass yet again.

Eager to make things right before the next day, he gathered up his equipment, congratulated the models on a great job, and said his farewells to the rest of the crew, who'd be stuck there for at least another hour cleaning up. Robert was waiting for him outside.

"All done, sir?"

"Yes. It was another successful shoot."

"And Ms. Allen?"

"She went home."

"Home, sir?"

Robert's accusing glare had him squirming where he stood. "Yes. She said she wasn't feeling well."

"Shall we take her some chicken soup?"

Leo laughed. "No."

They walked the remainder of the way to the limo in silence. Robert opened the door for Leo and cleared his throat. "To Ms. Allen's house, sir?"

"Did you even have to ask?" Leo said before sinking into the soft leather seat.

»»·««

Karen lived on the Upper East Side. *How on earth is she able to afford a place in this neighbourhood?* Was that why she never wanted him to take her home—so he wouldn't find out how well off she was? The house was a quaint brownstone with a navy-blue front door that made it stand out from the houses around it. A large holly berry wreath hung on the door, sending a splash of colour into the slush-covered street. Leaving the warmth of the limo, Leo walked up the three steps. Upon closer examination, the door actually looked a deep violet. He pressed the doorbell, which rang out the last few notes of "Carol of the Bells."

The door opened to reveal Karen wearing black yoga capris and a red tank top. Her skin glistened with sweat from her workout, and her blond hair was up in a high ponytail. He'd never been so turned on than at that moment.

Her look of surprise turned to annoyance in a matter of seconds. "What are you doing here? Better yet, how did you find me?"

She was pissed. That didn't bode well for his asking her out for dinner.

"Well, I did tell you I'd find you." *Okay, that might not have been the best approach to take,* he realised.

Her eyebrows shot up in response. "I'm sure whatever you have to say can wait until tomorrow."

"Actually, it can't."

Karen leaned against the doorjamb and closed the door a bit so he couldn't see inside. He was freezing. He'd foolishly left his jacket in the limo.

"May I come inside?"

From the sigh she exhaled, it sounded as if the worries of the world lay on her slight shoulders. She reluctantly opened the door wide and stepped aside.

Leo took in the white bare walls and single exposed light bulb that barely lit the foyer. A green gym bag sat in the corner, emitting a not-so-fabulous odour. To the right, a coat closet door barely hung from its top hinge. A black hoodie with a skull-and-crossbones pattern sat haphazardly on an old wire hanger. The lack of decor in the tiny space didn't bode well for the rest of the house. And didn't fit Karen's personality at all.

Karen disappeared around the corner, so Leo removed his shoes and followed. The rest of the first floor was open concept and as bare as the foyer. A matching brown futon couch and chair set, along with a rickety coffee table, took up the most space in the room, paying homage to a huge 4K screen television. The walls were bare aside from a small clock above the archway into the kitchen, which housed the basic necessities. Old pinstriped wallpaper was peeling off in spots and yellowish and faded in others.

"Umm...lovely place you have here."

Karen let out a choked laugh. "Oh, please. You're itching to run and wash the filth off your skin."

"You're not wrong," he said.

Karen's laugh filled the space and his heart. It felt so good to hear that sound from her. Her smile lit her face and put a sparkle in her eyes he hadn't seen since he'd taken her to bed all those years ago. His loins stirred thinking about her naked above him, her eyes sleepy with lust. It didn't help watching Karen now move around the room fluffing tacky animal-print throw pillows in those yoga pants.

"Would you like a drink?"

"Sure."

Karen disappeared into the tiny kitchen, and Leo took advantage of the privacy to scrutinize the couch, looking for dirt and spills.

"It's safe to sit. This place may look in a sorry state, but it's clean."

Leo took the glass of white wine Karen handed him and sipped the golden liquid. His eyebrows arched in surprise. "This is good...really good."

"Well, I hope so. This is the pinot gris from your family's California winery."

A flurry of emotions swirled in his chest, pride and surprise most prominent. This disturbed him, as he had no wish to pursue an interest in the family wineries.

"My parents know what they're doing." He sank onto the couch and sighed. "I'll give them that."

"And you have no desire to be part of the process that has made them such a success?"

Leo stood and ran his hands through his hair. "No."

"Why not? You seem to enjoy the fruits of your family's labour." She tipped her glass at him in mock salute.

Leo closed the space between them so only their wine glasses kept them apart. Heat vibrated off his body, stirring his loins yet again as Karen's gaze drifted to his lips. How he wanted to devour her, but he couldn't let her barb go unreturned. "Why don't you tell me the reason you're living in a dump? This isn't you."

Karen's eyes flashed with her anger before she stepped back. "Well played."

"I want an answer."

"As do I from you."

The seconds dragged as they stared at each other, neither willing to back down. The air was electrified between them, their breath deepening and Karen's breasts rising and falling in a hypnotic rhythm. She wanted him as much as he wanted her, he realised.

He lifted his free hand and caressed her cheek. Her sharp intake of breath had his heart racing. "You are so beautiful."

He placed a well-aimed kiss on the arch of her neck and made his way to her chin. Her moans encouraged him to go higher until their lips were locked together and feeding off each other.

Their wine glasses rattled between them, and before Leo could grab them, they fell onto the rug with a thud. Wine spilled everywhere.

"Oh no." Karen gasped. On her knees, she wiped at the liquid with her hands.

"Karen."

"This is a new rug. An expensive rug."

"Towels?"

"In the bottom drawer beside the stove."

Leo returned with a pile of towels and joined Karen in mopping up the mess.

"Thank goodness it wasn't red wine." His attempt at humour was met with a cold stare.

Leo sat back on his haunches and studied Karen as she mopped up the wine with a vengeance.

"So, what is a girl like you doing in a place like this?"

Karen stood, taking the wet towels with her. "Do you mean to ask why my place looks like I moved in and forgot to renovate?"

"You read my mind." Raising himself up, he took the towels from her. "Laundry?"

"Upstairs. Follow me."

Leo noticed the changes right away as he followed her to the back of the house and up the plush carpeted steps, which were framed with a beautiful wrought-iron railing, and down a brightly lit hallway. She slid open a glass sliding door to reveal a state-of-the-art matching washer and dryer set. The top level screamed modern decor and good taste. After tossing the towels inside, she ordered him to stay put and headed to another door at the end of the hallway. Curious now, he tagged along and pushed open the door she had left ajar.

The same vibe flowed into this room. Creamy walls were accented with pieces of cheap art in all colours of the rainbow. A canopied queen-size bed was centred in the space, with a matching set of nightstands and an armoire. There was nothing girly in this room—only sophisticated, fashionable woman. Gauzy scarves were draped over a chair and an oval full-sized mirror. In the corner stood a seamstress's dummy draped in black silk—a project underway?

"This is the Karen I remember."

Karen spun around and squealed. "Get out."

"Why? So you can shut me out even more?"

She crossed her arms and let out a frustrated huff. "Don't take it personally. No one is allowed in here."

"Meaning a possible roommate or a boyfriend?" His stomach constricted painfully at the thought.

"Yes."

Yes, what? She has a boyfriend. He turned around to mentally squash the little green monster that had popped up out of nowhere.

"This isn't my place," she revealed.

"Considering the state of the main floor, I'd say that's a relief."

Karen's mouth turned upward in a small grin. "I underestimated how hard it'd be to find something to rent. I was so in love with the thought of living in New York that I rushed here with no plans. I almost gave up and went back home. New York isn't for the weak of heart."

"No, it isn't." He stepped closer, wanting to touch her soft skin, but he didn't. "You're not weak."

"I was desperate."

"You didn't do something...sell yourself...?"

"Don't be ridiculous." Karen stepped back, breaking the intimacy building between them.

"Then what?"

"A high school friend is putting me up during my internship."

Must be some friend. "You lucked out. Space in the Big Apple is not so easy to come by."

"Apparently a prior roommate had moved out, and the room was mine if I wanted it."

"And what's your roommate's story? Why the lack of decor and upkeep downstairs?"

"Well..."

"And what exactly does your roommate do for a living?"

Karen's cheeks flushed under his interrogation.

"My roommate runs a video game den."

"A what?"

"A place where gamers come to hang out and play other serious gamers around the world."

A deep ache sat in the pit of his stomach. "Your roommate isn't your BFF from high school, is she?"

"Oh, quit running circles around the real issue, Leo. I'm living with a man, okay?"

It wasn't okay. It was anything but okay. A man who probably figured she owed him because he was providing her with a place to live. Meanwhile, she had to put up with a house full of men who eyed her like candy. *The Big Bang Theory* popped into his head at that thought.

"Come live with me," he blurted. *Had he said that?*

Karen's mouth dropped open. "Excuse me?"

Leo stepped in front of her and placed his hands on her shoulders. He couldn't take back what he'd said now no matter how much his heart thundered in his chest and his stomach constricted in protest. "You deserve better than this odd living situation. And it worries me that your professional gamer friend can afford to renovate the upstairs like a home off HGTV."

"Leo, don't be ridiculous. You're only here for a few more days. Besides, there's nothing illegal going on here. I'm renting a room in my friend's house. I'm barely here, and I really don't care if the kitchen appliances don't match or if the floor is laminate instead of hardwood."

"Karen, please..."

"Or if my lawyer friend has a gaming hobby in his spare time."

"Lawyer?" Leo couldn't have heard correctly.

"Yes, quite a successful lawyer, as a matter of fact."

"And when your internship ends…"

"I will deal with that when it comes."

"Karen—"

She stepped out of his grasp and gave a long sigh. "What did you come here to tell me, Leo?"

He'd almost forgotten. "I've come to invite you out tomorrow night."

"Invite me out? Is there a party I don't know about?"

"No. Supper—you and me. For Valentine's Day."

Her cheeks lit up and her eyes flashed. "No one else available? Did Natasha turn you down?"

"I didn't ask Nat. I'm asking you."

Karen marched past him and out the door. He followed her back downstairs, where she stood with the front door open. The brisk evening wind sent a chill right through him.

"You need to leave."

"I'm not leaving."

"What did you think was going to happen? Poor little Karen has no date, so I may as well take her, so she doesn't cry herself to sleep?"

"That's not what I said…"

Her eyes flashed with unleashed anger. "Just so you know, I already have a date. Someone who didn't wait until the night before to ask me out of pity. Good-bye, Leo."

Leo slipped his shoes on and walked back into the freezing winter night. The front door slammed shut behind him, and he winced at the sound as it vibrated in the cold air. Robert stood by the passenger door waiting to let him in with a "what have you done now?" look on his face. He really had no idea.

Chapter 6

"Monsieur St. Clare, welcome to Les Sens Bistro. Such a pleasure to have you here tonight."

"Thank you for fitting us in, Maurice."

The manager smiled and bowed his head. "My pleasure, monsieur."

Les Sens Bistro occupied a tiny space in an industrial building alongside a café, a barbershop, and a women's boutique in downtown Manhattan. The dining room seated twenty-eight people and had a scattering of booths for groups and single tables for couples. Tonight, the bistro's ambience oozed romance from the lit candles, the long stem red roses in tall glass vases to the music. Valentine's Day at this famous restaurant had been booked solid for six months, but when Leo had put a call in the other day a table had magically opened up for tonight's theme—a blindfold experience that was all the rage.

"I do, unfortunately, have one small issue..."

Leo was already in a pissy mood. He had no tolerance for more issues. "What is it?"

"As this is one of our busiest nights, we've tried to accommodate all of our guests. It is a bit cramped, so privacy is at a minimum."

"Aww, Leo, darling," Mindy whined as her grip on his arm tightened. "That's not romantic at all."

Leo gazed down at Mindy and wondered for the umpteenth time why he'd asked her out. Her face was heavily done up, her hair down and loose. She'd squeezed herself into a skintight nude-coloured dress with such low cleavage there was nothing left to the imagination. She was every inch the bombshell, and every man on the street outside the restaurant couldn't help but stare as they walked past.

She'd been so excited when he'd called her the night before that he hadn't had the heart to tell her this was a one-time thing. No romance. No desire. No sex. He just didn't want to be alone.

"The experience will be quite enjoyable once blindfolded, Monsieur St. Clare. A whole new awareness."

Leo turned his attention back to the maître d'. "Sounds great. And we want the whole experience, don't we, my dear?"

"Wonderful." Maurice clapped his hands then passed a menu to each of them. "Please peruse the menu at your leisure and then I'll escort you into the dining room."

After donning their blindfolds, they were led to their table. Conversation buzzed around them as the room began to fill up, and the sweet smell of vanilla and cinnamon filled the air as their remaining senses were heightened.

Their waiter seated them, placed napkins on their laps, and directed them on where their wine glasses and utensils were located. After a few sips of the zinfandel that had been poured in his glass to accompany the appetizers, he found conversation flowed freely—between the other two couples. Mindy sat stiffly beside him, her disappointment oozing off her as strong as whatever flowery perfume she wore. Perhaps it would've been better if he'd stayed home and nursed a nice glass of scotch instead.

Leo squeezed her elbow and whispered in her ear, "Cheer up, Mindy. You're acting like someone's died."

"I am not happy," she whined.

"Keep your voice down."

"I am." Her voice dripped with anger.

Leo sighed. This wasn't working. And in no way had he pictured the evening going like this. He'd figured on an excellent meal, some light conversation, and then a chaste kiss on her cheek before dropping her off at her friend's apartment. Perhaps he should suggest they leave. Maurice would understand.

"What do you—?"

"I'm going to the washroom," she interrupted and stood. The chair legs screeched along the floor like fingers on a chalkboard.

"I will escort you, mademoiselle," a male waiter said as he approached their table.

"Thank you."

Leo reached for his wine glass and downed the contents.

"Someone's not getting any tonight," one of the men at the table said, and the rest of the party laughed.

"Don't be rude, Paul. You probably won't either." A different male voice this time.

A distinct female laugh filled the air, followed by the clinking of glasses. Leo's senses went into hyper drive and his pulse started to race. He knew that laugh. But he had to be sure.

He lifted his wine glass, signalling for more.

A waiter appeared beside him. "More zinfandel, monsieur?"

He nodded.

"Do you want more zin, Karen?"

Leo's heart almost jumped out of his throat. It was her. What were the odds? There was no way he was leaving now.

"Yes, please." Karen's voice was soft but direct, a soothing balm to his bad mood. The waiter made his way around the table refilling wine glasses. "Will you be serving any wines from the St. Clare estate tonight?"

"Yes, mademoiselle. It is our most popular wine selection."

"Excellent."

Did she know he was here sitting only a few feet away? Impossible; he hadn't said a word above a whisper. Maybe she'd seen him on the way inside. No, he'd arrived early and received the VIP treatment to keep the paparazzi at bay.

"Monsieur?"

Leo tilted his face up as Maurice placed his hand on his shoulder and whispered, "Your date has left. Said she was not feeling well."

Leo removed his mask and motioned for some privacy. Before he followed Maurice back to the kitchen, he drank in the view of Karen laughing with her friends. Her cheeks were flushed from the wine and her neck was exposed perfectly for a row of intimate kisses. He couldn't see all of her dress, but the cleavage show her date would've gotten if he hadn't had his mask on burned a trail of unease to his stomach.

As they turned a corner near the kitchen, Maurice broke into speech, wringing his hands. "If you'd prefer, I can arrange a table for you, Monsieur St. Clare. I am so sorry about this. I will have my staff at your beck and call."

"I would like to finish my meal if you don't mind setting me up somewhere more private. I'll hang out for a bit and enjoy the atmosphere."

Maurice clapped his hands. "Oui." He turned and disappeared into the kitchen. "Michel. I need a table set up ASAP."

Leo's cosy new spot was more than ideal. He had the perfect spot to people-watch, having ditched the blindfold with Maurice's okay, but most importantly, to keep an eye on Karen. He'd wait patiently for her to pass by on the way to the washroom. He only needed a moment alone with her to satisfy the craving that refused to go away.

»»·««

Karen's cheeks burned pleasantly from both the wine and the laughter. Surprisingly, this double date had all the signs of being the best time she'd had since moving to New York. All the senses she took for granted on a regular basis were on full alert with the blindfold on. The food tasted exquisite; the spices perfect. Even in the wine she could taste all the different elements. Vanilla and cinnamon wafted up her nose, calming her.

But this all took second place to the company she shared. Her date, Paul, was a delight. Funny, smart, and witty, not to mention handsome; he really was the whole package.

Dessert arrived along with a bottle of sweet rosé.

"May I sit beside you?" Paul whispered in her ear.

When had he gotten up? "Sure." Her heart raced as Paul asked their waiter to position his chair beside hers. He squeezed in as close as he could, their thighs touching. He picked up her hand and placed it in his, sweeping his thumb back and forth in a hypnotic motion on the top of her hand. "You are quite suave."

Paul's laugh was deep and seductive. "It's easy with such a beautiful woman."

"Are you sure you're a lawyer?"

This time his laugh was genuine. "We're not all that bad."

Karen shrugged then remembered Paul couldn't see her. "That's to be determined."

Paul took her other hand and held both in his on the table.

"That sounds like a second date to me. Or maybe a nightcap?"

A nightcap? Karen knew Mike would be staying out late to enjoy his own nightcap with his date, Geoff, so the house would be empty...but to have Paul come over. Alone. Her thoughts flashed to the night before when Leo had followed her into her bedroom. Yes, she'd freaked out at first, but he'd dominated the space like he belonged. And that had scared her.

She tried picturing Paul there and couldn't. That scared her more.

Karen pushed her chair back and stood. She needed to get away, but Paul still had both her hands in his.

"What's wrong?" he asked.

"Oh, nothing...nothing. I need to use the washroom."

"Okay." He released her hands, and their waiter escorted her away from the table.

"The door is right here, mademoiselle. Please leave the blindfold on until you step inside."

"Thank you." The pressure on her elbow disappeared, and she reached out to push the door but was greeted with a solid wall.

"What the—?" Karen felt along the wall for a door and found nothing. *Is this some kind of joke?*

Warm hands grabbed her shoulders and turned her around.

"Thank you for coming. I can't seem to find the door. Really, you guys should have different rules about the washroom."

The hands left her shoulders and slid up her neck then cupped her cheeks.

"Umm..." This was totally inappropriate. She needed to scream...or something. Why couldn't she get a sound out?

But when firm, chiseled lips touched hers so gently and then parted hers to access her tongue, she almost swooned. She'd never been kissed with such heat, and then, as the kiss became more possessive and demanding...never with such passion. Her body arched forward, needing to touch, to feel the heat burn her skin. Fingers were in her hair now, massaging. Her fingers gripped jacket lapels and itched to slide around and find skin.

As the kiss slowed, her muddled brain cleared and panic set in. What on earth had gotten into her? This was wrong. She released her grip on the jacket and pushed away, her fingers lingering a bit over the rock-hard pecs beneath.

Stomping down the lust that consumed her, she ripped the blindfold off her eyes. No one was there...

Sounds from the kitchen intensified as she took in her surroundings. The bathroom door was a few feet away from where she stood. No one was in either direction in the hallway or around the corner. There was no way she'd imagined all that, though. Someone was playing games with her.

"Mademoiselle? Are you ready to be escorted back to your table?" The maître d' turned the corner from the kitchen with his arm proffered.

"I...um...not yet. I got a bit lost and couldn't find the washroom. That's why I took my blindfold off."

"Did your waiter not inform you that, once in this hallway, you are to remove it?"

"No."

"Oh, dear. My apologies, mademoiselle. I will wait for you right here and escort you personally back to your table."

"I'd appreciate that, thank you."

Karen dashed into the washroom thankful it was empty.

Am I going crazy? she thought as she washed her hands and splashed some cold water on her heated cheeks. The kiss and the rock-hard pecs had been real. They had to be. She'd never been kissed like that before, even by Leo. But she'd felt safe, like she'd belonged in that embrace. And that made no sense. It couldn't have been Leo. He had no idea she'd be there tonight, and New York was no tiny town.

Had it been Paul? She had to find out.

Back at her table, when Karen had her blindfold back on, Mike offered her a glass of the dessert wine, which she downed immediately.

"You okay?"

"Where's Paul?" She asked.

"Washroom."

Karen's stomach contracted and she gasped. "You're sure?"

"Yeah. He followed you there. You didn't see him?"

Karen lowered her chin. "It was him." And that revelation brought no excitement, only worry.

"You did see him?"

Karen heard his confusion. "I didn't see him. I felt him. He kissed me while I was still blindfolded...and it was wonderful."

"And this is apparently a big problem," Mike said with a chuckle and shared a glance with Geoff.

She didn't want it to be a problem. She needed to move on from her old feelings for Leo, but the disappointment sat so heavy around her heart that she wanted to cry.

"I'm done for the night, Mike. I'm going to catch a cab home. It was so nice to meet you, Geoff." She stood and signalled for a waiter.

"What should I tell Paul?"

"To call me tomorrow."

Yes, perhaps after a good night's sleep she'd feel better able to deal with these conflicting emotions. Not caring about restaurant protocol any longer, she removed her blindfold, grabbed her purse and coat, and left.

»»·««

The breathtaking view from Natasha's office always surprised Karen. This morning's sky had traces of pink and orange with barely a cloud in sight, which called for a cold and brisk day.

A steaming cup of coffee sat on Natasha's desk, and Karen held her own in front of her, enjoying the warmth that radiated into her hands. The previous night's kiss at Les Sens replayed in her mind yet again. She'd gotten no sleep and was living off her third cup of coffee already. The jitters were kicking in, and she welcomed the racing thoughts about what her day would bring. Anything to stop thinking about that bone-melting kiss...and that it hadn't been Leo who'd given it to her.

"Oh, grow up, Karen," she said to herself.

"I never thought I'd ever agree with you." Karen turned to find Natasha removing her coat. She tossed it onto the couch then grabbed her coffee. She took a sip and smiled. "You got it right this morning."

"I know."

Natasha sent her a cool sideways glance. "You're in a foul mood."

Karen met her stare with a questioning one. "And you're in a good mood. Weird."

Natasha flicked her hair behind her shoulder and turned toward her desk. "I had an excellent night. I love Valentine's Day."

I love Valentine's Day, Karen's mind mimicked as her head moved back and forth with each syllable.

"Your mouth is in overdrive again. Take your bad mood for a walk and get me something sweet for breakfast."

Karen sighed. "Any preference?"

"Surprise me."

"Seriously?"

"Knock, knock."

Karen turned to see Leo leaning against the doorjamb, his muscled arms crossed at his chest and the most mischievous grin on his face. She hoped she wasn't drooling.

"Oh, Leo." Natasha squealed and ran to him. She practically jumped into his arms, causing them to fall backward a few steps.

Leo's gaze met Karen's, and she detected a flash of guilt. Had he lied about him and Natasha? Had he spent last night with her? She hadn't thought her heart could feel so heavy.

"Last night was absolutely amazing. So many surprises to keep me on my toes."

Karen took a sip of her coffee. It had gone cold...as she had.

"I'll leave you two to reminisce," Karen said, and she made to leave, but Leo grabbed her elbow.

"Don't go."

"I don't need to be here."

"You do." Holding both hers and Natasha's elbows, he escorted them to the couch. "Sit."

"Really, Leo," Natasha said as he pushed her down.

"I will not—" Karen remained firm and escaped his grasp.

"You two really have to work out your issues."

"We have no issues," Karen argued.

Leo gave her a leveled gaze. "If you say so." He turned his attention to Natasha and said, "I need to borrow Karen today. I got called for a reshoot."

Natasha tilted her head in question. "You never have to do a reshoot."

Even Karen had to admit what he'd said didn't jive.

"Thanks, but I was on my own for a good chunk of yesterday and it shows."

Natasha looked at Karen. "What happened?"

He'd thrown her under the bus again, she realised. Another strike against him. She really needed to move on.

"I wasn't feeling well, and the session was pretty much finished..."

Natasha stood and squared her shoulders, all business now. "Apparently not. You owe Leo your time."

"What about your to-do list?" Karen asked as Leo stood by and had the audacity to grin. She needed the mind-dulling list of never-ending items to keep her mind off Leo—not to be stuck at his side.

"Finish it when you get back. It's overtime for you today." Natasha sat and took a sip of her coffee. "Ugh. This is freezing cold. Get me a new one as well as a sweet breakfast...before you go." She flicked her hand at them in dismissal before picking up the phone receiver and barking orders at the poor soul on the other end.

»»·««

"Where's Robert?" The wind whipped and howled through the tall buildings as they stood on the sidewalk.

"Robert is taking a well-deserved day off."

A red Porsche pulled up beside them. The door opened, and Leo stepped forward to place a wad of bills in the young man's outstretched hand.

"This is your car." A rush of old memories and excitement ran up her spine.

"You remember." He glanced at her quickly and then opened the tiny trunk and gently placed his camera equipment inside. Karen added her messenger bag and then let herself into the passenger side.

She sank into the soft tan leather seat and gave a sigh of pleasure. Leo got in the driver's seat, turned the key in the ignition, and blasted the heat.

"You look good sitting there," he said.

Their eyes met, and time drifted back to their college days.

"And you're still the suave playboy looking for a good time in your sexy car."

Leo grinned and bumped the gearshift into drive. "It was only ever you who thought I was a playboy." Besides, all good things happen in a sexy car."

"According to you, yes."

Silence filled the small space as they drove farther away from Vale Designs, and what surprised her was the relief mingled with excitement. Not the fear, anxiety, and dread of being stuck with Leo for a whole day.

Feeling a bit playful, Karen started turning dials and opening compartments.

"Karen..."

"Yes?" She batted her eyelashes and smiled. She knew he was going crazy. Nobody was allowed to touch anything in his car.

"You know the rules."

"What rules?"

"No touching."

"Well, it's a silly rule. Always has been."

"Silly. Really?"

Karen turned in her seat to face him. "Yes, really. Technically I am the navigator, so when you have both hands on the wheel—"

"One hand on the wheel, one on the gear shift."

"Exactly. Don't interrupt." She slapped his leg.

Leo grabbed her wrist with lightning speed. "Be careful." His voice hissed out the warning, but his eyes promised her things she was afraid to think about.

"Eyes on the road." Her voice was a raspy whisper.

Leo looked at her for a few more seconds then did as she asked. "And as my navigator?"

Grateful for the question, Karen leaned forward. "I'm in charge of temperature control and music." Leo grunted. "Come on. I promise I won't break anything."

"There are rules for a reason."

"Aren't rules meant to be broken?"

Leo jolted the steering wheel to the right and pulled the car over on the side of the street.

"What are you doing?" Karen yelped.

He knocked the gear into neutral to park then undid his seatbelt.

"If rules are meant to be broken, then this will be allowed at all times." He reached over and pulled her as far forward as her seatbelt allowed and kissed her— long, hard, and quite thoroughly.

Karen drowned in the sensations as they swirled from her head down to her toes. If she hadn't already been sitting, she would've fallen. As if they had a mind of their own, her hands reached up to caress the back of his neck, her fingers entwined in his hair. Their bodies were too far apart. *Damn seatbelt.*

As if reading her mind, Leo undid her buckle, and she crawled over the console into his lap, not breaking the kiss for one moment. All she wanted was the sensation of this pure kiss, with all reason thrown out the window. Not giving consequences a second thought, she would have taken him right there in his sexy red car with no protection between them. She craved it more than anything else in the world.

This kiss matched the one Paul had given her at Les Sens the night before... *Damn.*

Karen pulled away, her head down. Why on earth would she think about Paul at a time like this? The feather-light tingling sensation was replaced by a heavy rock in the pit of her stomach.

Leo tilted her head up, forcing her to look at him. "What's going on?"

Things had been going so well, and the day was still young. "Nothing."

He let go of her and sat back. "Liar."

Karen moved back into her seat and buckled up.

Better for him to think her a liar than tell him she was comparing his kiss to another man's. The worst of it was her mind wanted Paul—handsome, successful, and funny—but her heart wanted Leo—the one who'd already broken her heart once and refused to grow up and accept responsibility. She needed to go forward, not backward.

"Some rules shouldn't be broken."

"I suppose not."

Back on the road, the silence grew deafening. Karen itched to turn on the radio but decided against it and looked out the window instead. They were heading out of town. *What the hell?*

"Where are we going? I thought we had to reshoot at Rockefeller?"

Leo didn't say anything right away. When he did, he kept his eyes focused on the road. "There is no reshoot."

"Pardon?"

"We're headed to the Hudson Valley."

Had Karen heard him correctly? The Hudson Valley was a good two hours away. Panic set in as she pictured Natasha screeching like a banshee before firing her on the spot.

"Leo, we can't go out of town."

"And why not?"

"I owe you some hours and have a huge Ms. Nasty Vale list to get through before the end of the day."

"You don't owe me any hours, Karen."

"But…"

"And I'll have you back with plenty of time to at least tackle most of Nat's nasty list."

"Gee, thanks," Karen said.

"My pleasure."

Karen couldn't help smiling. "You lied to Natasha and me for what reason?"

"I need another pair of eyes."

"I do have those."

Leo laughed as he steered the car toward the ramp and headed north.

"Are we checking out spots for future shoots?"

"Something like that."

"Okay, Mister Mysterious. I won't ask any more questions…for now. But…" She flicked the radio on, and "Crazy" by Aerosmith filled the space between them. "This means I get my full navigator duties reinstated."

Leo grunted again.

"Go team," Karen said, and she started singing along with the radio.

»»•««

The two-hour car ride whizzed by as they sang along to the Classic Rewind station. It had started to drizzle an hour into the trip then turned into heavy, wet sleet. Leo had slowed down, and the windshield wipers were going at full speed. Karen concentrated on the scenery as it changed from city to farmland with occasional rows of vines. Depending on the size of the winery, some of the estates towered over the fields like Scottish castles, but more were homey cottages.

Leo turned onto a gravel road with a "For Sale" sign posted in the ditch. Huge sycamore trees arched over the road like a covered bridge, and after a few minutes they emerged into a wide yard with a huge cement water fountain as the dominant feature. Behind the fountain monstrosity, a cute little two-story cottage was nestled among a variety of bare shrubs. An "Open" sign flashed in the front window.

"How charming," Karen exclaimed as Leo pulled into a parking spot. Her mind went into instant work mode as it played with scenes, colours, and models who would best bring out the striking character of the place.

"Yes," Leo agreed reluctantly, and he got out of the car.

The rain refused to let up as they dashed inside. Karen wiped her boots on the welcome mat and stepped up to the desk.

"Leo, this is a B&B."

"Yes... Interesting."

An elderly lady emerged from a back room to greet them. Pleasantly plump, she wore a bespeckled denim jumpsuit and a short apron around her waist. Her grey hair sat in a loose bun on top of her head and her cheeks were dusted with flour.

"Welcome to Happy Haven Bed and Breakfast. I'm Bea. Do you have a reservation?"

"No," Leo answered. "I saw the for-sale sign at the end of the drive."

Bea wiped her hands on her apron and took a step closer. She eyed Leo up and down and then rang the desk bell three times. "You're interested in this old place?"

A man wearing mud-covered coveralls and a faded baseball hat came in through a side door. "You rang, Ma?"

Bea nodded. "This here is Walter, my husband. You can talk to him about such business." Dismissing them, she walked back through the door she'd come in.

Karen didn't know what was going on. Here she'd been in full work mode, staging shoots and scribbling in her notepad, when Leo had blurted out "for-sale sign."

"I can give ya the tour," Walter announced as he shuffled his feet, apparently in no hurry to help them out.

"I'd appreciate a tour of the building," Leo said. "Karen, can you take notes?"

"Umm...sure."

The cottage itself was bigger than it had looked from the outside. Once they left the front foyer, they entered a huge living space with a roaring fire and overstuffed furniture. "Cozy" came to Karen's mind. The kitchen at the back of the house was small but fully equipped to host guests. A set of narrow stairs took them up to a master bedroom with its own en-suite bathroom, plus three other small bedrooms with a bathroom in the hallway for the guests to share. *Not ideal*, Karen scribbled in her notepad.

After the tour, Walter showed them back to the foyer, leaving them alone.

"I've never been involved in such detailed shoot scouting," Karen said, breaking the silence. She opened her notepad to the beginning of her notes. "So, I'm going to assume this isn't for a shoot either."

Leo glanced over at her and sighed. "Right again."

"What's going on here, Leo? Why all the secrecy today?"

He paced in front of the desk, his stance hunched and his feet dragging. Boy, he was struggling.

"My parents wanted me to check this place out. They're thinking about buying it."

Karen's notepad slipped out of her hands. "You...the family business? No way."

"Only as a favour. I'm here anyway," he spat out.

She couldn't believe it. He was doing something for his family. *But...* "This isn't a winery, Leo."

"It could be," he sighed.

Chapter 7

Leo knew this was a bad idea. He didn't want to be sucked into the family business. It had ruined his parents' marriage, consumed all of his brother's time, and his sister...well, if his parents had been home more instead of gallivanting around the world in their quest for success, she wouldn't have been left alone with an eighteen-year-old who detested being stuck baby-sitting...and in the end had failed her; failed them all. He'd vowed never to take responsibility for anyone else again.

But...an unfamiliar excitement buzzed in his belly, different from his usual forms of pleasure—drag racing, poker games, and women. Those things brought him intense desperation, a wild urge for speed, chance, and self-satisfaction. But this...he'd never felt this way before.

Leo's gaze drank in the gold wallpaper, dark wood, and bright overhead lights in the foyer. His photographer's eye saw the potential in this out-of-date B&B. And heaven help him, he wanted it. Giddiness he hadn't experienced since Christmas morning in his childhood swept through him, and he had the sudden urge to dance a jig.

"What do you mean it could be a winery?"

Karen's voice was barely a whisper, but he heard it through the buzzing in his ears.

"Can't you see it?" he asked, and he swept his arms in a wide arc to indicate the room. "Customers will enter through grand double doors into a foyer with a vaulted ceiling and rows upon rows of estate wine. One door will lead out to the vineyard for tours, and another will lead to a huge living space, a common area, where customers staying overnight can hang out and enjoy the evenings. A spiral staircase will lead up to the bedrooms, each with an en-suite and a balcony facing the vineyard."

It clicked together so clearly, like putting the final piece in a puzzle.

"I want this, Karen."

"And, therefore, you shall have it."

A bit of the excitement was knocked out of him by her sarcastic comment. "What do you mean?"

"It means exactly what I said. You always get what you want."

Leo closed the space between them. He hovered a few inches away but didn't touch her. The green flecks in her eyes darkened in a matter of moments. "Not everything."

Karen stepped back, and the spell was broken. "Perhaps not, but this is a passing fancy, a new toy for Mr. St. Clare to add to his collection."

"No."

"Tell me, do you want this for you or for the family business?"

"The family business. What on earth would I do with a winery?" Prickles of doubt crept across his skin when he considered her questions. Like in college, she got under his skin and made him doubt himself. No one had been able to come so close to the truth but her.

"Is there even a decent vineyard here?" Karen asked, bringing him back to the present.

"We have vines," Walter said as he entered the room.

"I'd like to see them." Leo zipped up his coat and headed toward the door.

"Not possible."

"Why not?" he snapped.

"The storm brewing all day is here."

Leo went to the window and pulled the curtain back. It was snowing so hard he couldn't even see the car. Karen joined him at the window and wrapped her arms tight around herself. He noticed her slight shiver and made to put an arm around her shoulders, but she stepped away.

"I need to call Natasha." Karen dug into her purse for her cell phone.

"There is no cell service or Internet here," Walter said.

"What about the landline?" Karen asked.

"Dead for the last hour."

Karen groaned. "Great...I didn't even realise places were off the grid anymore."

"It's a great feature," Leo piped up. "Makes the B&B experience more intimate."

"It also makes it difficult to make reservations," Karen shot back.

"A minor detail," Leo said with a smile.

Karen glared daggers at him. "She's going to fire me if I don't report in."

"Oh, come on, Karen..."

She turned to face him, her arms stiff at her side. "Is this some kind of joke to you? All you have to do is flex your muscles and Natasha will melt into your arms and all will be forgiven. Can't you see how important this job is to me and how she'll blame me for all your lies?"

"I'll explain everything."

"Yeah, like all the other times. You're only about saving yourself."

Her observation cut right to his heart, and Leo had to take a deep breath to steady his racing pulse.

"I did not order this storm." As usual, his defence mechanism cut in.

"Did you check the weather before we left?" Karen shot back.

Shit. He really hadn't thought this through.

Leo turned to face Walter. "Do you have any idea when this storm will let up?"

"According to the news broadcast in the kitchen, not until morning."

Behind him, Karen groaned, and his guilt dug a deeper hole in the pit of his stomach.

"Do you have any rooms available for the night?"

Walter flipped through a worn ledger behind the desk. "We are booked up. Only three rooms—"

There was no way his Porsche would make it through all the snow. "Is there a nearby motel?"

"Not for many miles. Driving would be dangerous." Walter said with a disapproving frown.

"The living room, then."

Karen squeaked. "What?"

"I will pay you for the living room, but I want complete privacy from the other guests."

"Not possible—" Walter started.

"Then your bedroom. I will pay you ten thousand dollars for the night."

"I...um..."

Leo could see the moment the dollar amounts registered.

"Let me tidy up for you. Come, have some tea." Walter dashed out of the room. "Ma, make some tea."

"Impressive," Karen admitted. She hovered near the small fireplace in the corner. The fire looked about to go out.

Leo grabbed two pieces of wood from the basket and placed them on the fire. With a bit of coaxing, it sprang to life, and Karen sighed with relief.

"Thanks."

"No problem."

Silence stretched between them but for the clanging of dishes in the next room.

"Are we really going to do this?" Her gaze never left the flames as they danced in the grate.

"Well, we either share a room in this cosy B&B or we sleep in the car."

"But you're kicking an elderly couple out of their bedroom. Where will they sleep?"

"I'm sure they have an emergency pull-out couch somewhere."

"Then we should take it."

"The deal is already made. Besides, I like my privacy."

Karen's cheeks flushed a deep red. She stole a glance at him, and he grinned.

"You're seriously considering the car, aren't you?"

"Maybe for you." She stifled a laugh at his look of shock. "Come on. Our tea is going to get cold, and I want to hear about the vision you have for this place." The look of worry in her eyes didn't match the forced happiness of her voice.

He realised then he'd rather have her screeching mad than see her sad and disappointed look. He wasn't looking forward to tomorrow, but tonight he could make sure they forgot all about it.

»»•««

A fire burned pleasantly in the grate as they sipped their tea. Leo had pulled two armchairs close to the fire with an end table between them creating a cosy setting. It made such a domesticated scene, sitting there with the man her heart couldn't let go of with a storm in full force outside.

Her stomach growled, but Karen didn't know if it was from hunger or nerves. She knew without a doubt she'd be out of a job when they returned to the city, and the thought made her nauseous. What on earth would she do? What would she tell Anna?

Yet, even with all the mounting stress, her thoughts kept drifting to later, when they would be sharing a bedroom...and maybe a bed. No. The heartache she could do without.

But she admired him nonetheless over the rim of her teacup. His dark hair was dishevelled from the number of times he'd run his hands through it. He'd taken off his jacket and sweater and wore a light grey short-sleeve T-shirt which clung to him like a second skin. She itched to trace her fingers along his six-pack and the biceps.

"You look a bit flushed. If you want, I can move the chairs farther away from the fire."

Karen's gaze darted from his well-toned arms to his face. His eyes sparkled with mischief.

"I'm fine," she said, and she took another sip of tea.

"Yes, you are."

"Leo."

He smiled and reclined in his chair like a man with no worries in the world. "Well, I'm not blind. Your sweater dress leaves little to the imagination."

"This outfit is work conservative," she defended as she put down her cup and tried to stretch the dress to her knees.

"Please don't." His voice took on a sultry tone, and Karen was sure her knees turned as red as her cheeks.

She had to change the subject before she turned into a big pile of goo and slid to the floor. "Quit it," she said then more firmly, "And quit stalling."

"What do you mean?" Leo took another sip of his tea, his gaze still focused on her legs.

"I want to know what's going on with you, with this place."

"Nothing is going on with me." He stood, grabbed a piece of wood, and placed it on the fire. Instead of sitting back down, he paced in the small space between them. He reminded Karen of a caged lion.

"Why this sudden change of heart about your parents' business?"

Leo ran a hand through his hair and down the side of his neck, where he massaged his neck. "I'm helping them out of a bind. Mom and Dad are in France and my brother is in California, but they're interested in a property in New York. As I am in said location, it made sense to call me in."

The words coming out of his mouth sounded true, yet Karen noticed an internal struggle she'd never associated with Leo before. Had he really agreed to help his parents out? Or was he settling a personal score? Perhaps he meant to steal this from under his parents' well-meaning noses?

Karen concentrated on the bitterness of her tea, so she didn't have to dwell longer on those thoughts.

Walter's large frame filled the doorway. "We've arranged a private dinner for you in the formal dining room," he announced. "Please follow me."

"Thank you, Walter."

"I don't remember seeing a formal dining room," Leo observed as they followed Walter down the hallway.

"He wasn't overly excited to show you the place," Karen reminded Leo. "He could've easily skipped it during the tour."

"Right."

Walter led them down a long, winding hallway. At the end of the hall, double doors stood open to reveal a six-person table in front of a roaring fire. Textured wallpaper covered the walls, and heavy burgundy velvet drapes hung from ceiling-high windows. Beneath their feet, the cream-coloured carpet was worn and dirty from years of use.

Karen stood next to the table and admired the old blue and white chinaware. The wine goblets were already full of a full-bodied red, and a basket of buns and creamy butter sat in the middle of the table.

"What's for dinner, Walter?" Leo asked.

Walter cleared his throat. "Ma's famous garden salad and ravioli."

"Sounds wonderful," Karen said. "We can't wait."

Walter nodded and left.

"A toast then?" Leo picked up a wine glass, sniffed, swirled, and held it up to the light.

Karen followed suit and then raised her glass to him. "To a gentle storm and safe travels."

They clinked their glasses, but before they sipped, Leo added, "To a warm fire, a warm bed, and a long night."

Karen's cheeks burned under his sultry stare, and she sipped long and hard. The wine burned down her throat, settling comfortably in her belly. The lingering taste on her tongue was quite delightful.

"This wine is quite good."

Leo nodded. "It is, isn't it?"

He pulled out a chair for Karen and she sat. The other place setting was at the opposite end, but Leo gathered up each piece and set the space beside Karen creating an intimate atmosphere.

"If the wine they are turning out is this good in all the barrels, it might be worth it to go in at top dollar."

"Definitely."

"My parents will be thrilled."

"Probably."

"The wine could even be altered a bit to really be a hit and get this place on the map."

"Won't your parents want to have their own wine at the B&B?"

"Yes, they'd have bottles shipped here, but these vines will be different from the others—stronger, more durable and resilient in this type of weather. A different wine. A rebel..."

Karen visualized the gears turning in Leo's head. He genuinely seemed excited about this project for his parents. After Fashion Week was over, he'd have a new pet project to keep him busy and perhaps keep him in New York longer. A quick ripple of excitement shot through her, but then it died off. As of tomorrow, she might not have a job, and, knowing Natasha, she'd make sure Karen couldn't get a job anywhere else in town. She'd be better off to book her flight back home as soon as she could. She could always play it safe and take an internship in Vancouver, closer to home and Anna.

"You could, but you won't get the recognition you need."

Karen looked up from the pattern on the plate she'd been admiring. "Talking out loud again?"

"Yes." Leo took her hands, and sensation zipped along her spine, making her shiver.

"Sorry."

"Don't be. I get it. Being safe is, well, safe. Something I'm an expert at. I've been doing it for far too long. It's time for a change."

Karen let her gaze drift across his face. "Is that why you took the Fashion Week job?"

"One of the reasons. I was antsy, and photography to me is like designing for you. It just is."

Karen understood perfectly.

"Coming to New York wasn't for the models and the parties?"

Leo released one of her hands to take a sip of wine. "I'd be lying if I said no. At the time of the call, I'd been bored, restless, and desperate to seek out some fun. The gig took second place."

"And when did the gig take precedence?"

"The moment I saw you again."

Karen swallowed the lump in her throat. "Really?"

"I was a shadow of myself, going through the motions ever since college. You brought me back to life."

Karen's breath hitched. This was not the Leo St. Clare she remembered. He never would have admitted to such intimate emotions. But acknowledging them would only get her hopes up, and was something she had no interest in.

Yet her stubborn head had to have an answer to the one question which had haunted her since college, even though her heart screamed it didn't matter anymore.

She took a deep breath to steady her racing heart and looked down at her hands entwined on her lap. She could do this. Looking up at Leo, she blurted, "What had you so shaken up in college for you to turn our budding relationship into a one-night stand so we wouldn't speak again until five years later?"

Leo's eyes narrowed to slits and his mouth creased into a deep frown. He rose so quickly his chair caught on the carpet and toppled over.

In her attempt to catch the chair, she knocked her wine glass over, the red liquid instantly staining the white tablecloth. "Dammit."

"The salad is ready," Walter said as he walked in with two small plates and placed them between the cutlery.

Karen saw his look of surprise at the stain and immediately started apologising. "Walter, I am so sorry. I can take it and start soaking it for you."

"No, no. Ma will know what to do. I will leave for now."

Once Karen and Leo were alone again, the awkwardness between them was heightened.

"Let's eat," Leo suggested.

"Fine."

Karen sat and pulled her chair closer to the table as Leo picked up his chair. He poured more wine into her glass and topped his off.

The strained silence between them was almost unbearable save for the crackling fire. She'd put her fear aside to get answers which had haunted her for so long, and what had she gotten for it? The silent treatment. She'd rather be yelling and screaming at him. *Or kissing him.*

She chanced a quick glance at Leo to see if she'd said it aloud, but he was busy tossing his salad in between bites. Karen exhaled a sigh of relief and started pushing her salad around the plate, her appetite gone.

"Don't like it?" Leo asked.

"Oh, I'm sure it's fine." Karen forced herself to take a bite and raised her eyebrows in surprise. "This is really good."

"So far it's two for two." Leo took a big sip of his wine then got up and stood by the fire.

"Perhaps you could get her recipes."

"Already ahead of you." Leo turned and grinned at her before raising his glass in salute.

Karen hated to wreck the return of their easy mood, but they needed to talk. She needed to know before her circumstances sent her away from him.

"We need to talk about this."

"We don't."

"Leo, come on. You ending our friendship and disappearing after what I'd thought was a wonderful night has been the cause of a good chunk of my issues right now."

"Don't blame me for your insecurities."

"Oh, not all of them. But what is a girl to think about her sexuality, about herself as a woman and her attractiveness, when the man she cares about walks away?"

Leo stared into the fire; a frown so fierce on his face Karen thought he might start to scream.

"Growing up wasn't easy for me," she continued. "I had a lanky athletic body and boy-short hair which put me in the path of every bully in school. I wasn't pretty or popular no matter that I excelled in sports."

"Karen..."

"When I finally got a bit of confidence, due to a sexy guy at college who actually liked me *for me*, it made all the heartache worth it." She turned away from him and the warmness of the fire. "But you turned out to be the worst one of all, didn't you?" She could feel tears forming in the corners of her eyes and swiped them away briskly. "I don't know what I did to make you run...and

I don't care anymore. I need to get my confidence back and quit living in the past." *Waiting for you.*

His hands were on her shoulders, turning her to face him. "You were waiting for me?"

Karen closed her eyes. She had to stop verbalizing her thoughts. "No."

"But you said—"

"Well, I say a lot of things I don't mean."

Leo tilted her chin upward. "Liar."

Karen sighed in frustration, but then her lips quivered when he placed his only inches away...reminding her of another kiss. Another man.

"I *was* waiting for you, but no longer. I've found another."

Leo kissed her lips ever so lightly then smiled. "Oh really?"

Karen tried to steady her shaky legs. "Um...yes."

"And who is this someone? Have you known him for a long time?"

Leo wrapped his arms around her, and she found it disconcerting. *What is he playing at now?*

"We haven't known each other long." Her words rushed out at the look of surprise on his handsome features.

"He was the guy I went out with on Valentine's Day."

"Yesterday? You're moving on with a guy you went out with yesterday?"

Karen broke free from his embrace and took a big sip of wine, being careful not to knock it over again. "You make it sound so cheap."

"I guess I expected better of you."

Karen spun around; hands clenched at her sides. "How dare you."

"The main course is ready." Walter's voice drifted in from the hallway.

"Great," Karen said under her breath. "Walter probably heard everything."

"I'll be sure to leave a huge tip."

"Because money cures wagging tongues?"

"Not always, but Walter is a good guy."

Karen smiled when Walter walked in with two trays. "Smells divine, Walter."

"Ma went all out."

"Our warmest regards to the chef," Leo said as they sat at the table.

They tucked into the lobster ravioli, and Karen moaned with delight. "This is the best meal I've ever had."

Walter's cheeks turned a bright red. "Ma will be pleased." He refilled their wine glasses and took his leave, but not before advising them dessert would be chocolate cherry cheesecake with a dessert wine.

"If Bea is retiring, you must keep in touch, or I'll figure out a way to bring her home with me. Her food is to die for." Karen sighed before scooping another bite of ravioli into her mouth.

Leo laughed. "I will do my best."

Changing the subject helped them both calm down, as they talked more about Leo's vision for the B&B. Karen couldn't help the excitement building in her chest. He sounded genuinely happy and had some amazing ideas. But as they shared a cosy loveseat in front of the fire eating the last few bites of cheesecake, she knew she had to establish boundaries for them and move forward as friends.

"I'm going to go out with Paul again."

Leo pulled his gaze away from the fire. "Paul?" He dragged out the syllable.

"Yes. My Valentine's Day date."

"Right."

"I would like you and me to remain friends."

"Me too."

Karen nodded. "Good." *Easy peasy.*

Then why did she have a dull ache in her gut and a huge inclination to cry?

She downed the rest of her wine then placed the glass on the side table with a clang. Expecting a reprimand from Leo about being more careful, she didn't expect his next words.

"I was in a bad place back then." Leo's voice barely rose above a whisper.

"What?"

"I had a concrete shell around me which kept me safe...kept me sane."

Karen turned to face Leo then inched closer. Was he about to confide in her?

"And it worked great...until you came along. You grew on me and I let my guard down. My walls started to crumble and soon I was vulnerable again. But as is your way, you asked one too many questions...or possibly the one question I couldn't answer."

Karen remembered that day like it had happened only moments ago. It had been an unusually hot spring day, and they'd been on the beach sun tanning. Leo had been rubbing suntan lotion on her back. She'd been so relaxed, so happy, and so sure of her feelings for this man and the place she'd made in this college world of hers; her words had flowed from her like a waterfall. She'd wanted to know everything about Leo, from his favourite colour to his most embarrassing moment.

It'd been when she'd started asking questions about his family when she noticed a change in his mood and tone. She left it alone, and when they'd returned to his dorm room, they made passionate love. In her sated afterglow she'd resumed her questions, forgetting how upset Leo had been on the beach. When she'd woken late the next morning, it'd been to a cold bed and then a walk of shame past his buddies.

"What question did I ask?"

"It was so long ago, Karen. Why do you still want to know?"

"Why won't you tell me?" she snapped back.

"I honestly can't remember."

"Now who's the liar?"

Leo grabbed her arm and pulled her into his lap. "You are."

"I am not."

"And your delusional future with Paul?"

Karen opened her mouth, but nothing came out.

"No delusions," she finally managed to say. "He kissed me, and I knew."

"He kissed you, did he?"

Karen nodded, her gaze never leaving his.

"Did he kiss you like this?" Leo's mouth swooped down on hers and she was lost.

»»·««

His kiss was rough, and he knew it. She squirmed in his arms a bit, but he refused to let her go. Did she really believe it had been Paul who'd kissed her the night before in the restaurant? A strong possessiveness took hold, along with the irrational thought that she should've known.

And who moved on with a man because of his kiss? His grip on her upper arms increased, and she moaned against his lips. No, he didn't want to punish her; he wanted her to realise who her mystery man really was and then decide who she wanted to be with.

Softening the pressure of his lips, Leo ran his tongue along Karen's full bottom lip and then dipped inside to start a slow tangle with her tongue. She tasted delicious, with hints of chocolate and cherry. Concentrating on the intoxicating combination, he deepened the kiss and pressed his body closer to hers.

Leaving her luscious mouth, he kissed a trail down her neck. Her pulse raced, and out of the corner of his eye he could see her chest rising and falling with her laboured breaths. He ran his hands up her arms and her neck and then into her hair. He looked into her green eyes and saw the moment she realised the truth. Then he saw the confusion...and something else he couldn't quite name.

Abandoning all common sense, he began his seduction by lowering her to the rug in front of the fire. The fire spat and crackled, but it dimmed in comparison to the roaring in his ears. He had to have her—now.

"Leo," she breathed.

"Shhh..." Facing the fire, he lay beside her to shield her body from prying eyes. He ran his hand down the length of her body, spending extra time on her breasts and hips. With each pass of his hand, her dress rose higher and higher up her thighs. In no time at all he saw her pink lace panties, and he caressed the edges ever so gently. Karen's body wiggled beside him in response.

"We shouldn't..." she began, and she closed her eyes as his hand made its way up her stomach to linger below her bra line.

"Oh, we definitely should," he whispered in her ear before kissing the delicate flesh.

She shivered under his touch, and his heart soared with excitement as his eyes glazed over in lust. Karen had no reason to lack confidence—not where her body was concerned. She was a piece of art. Slim and toned, with a tiny waist and beautiful breasts cupped perfectly in a matching pink lace bra.

Karen watched him with a gaze quite bold and daring, and he wanted to know if her hands and lips would be as bold. He took hold of one of her hands and placed it on his hip. As he'd hoped, she squeezed and inched her way to his groin. He gritted his teeth and took a deep breath. He didn't know how much longer he could continue this seduction.

Karen sat up and pushed him down when he tried to join her. "My turn."

Leo gulped as her hands roamed over his clothes. She undid his belt, followed by his pant zipper and button. In one swift movement, she straddled his hips, and her hands were under his T-shirt tracing his abs. She leaned forward, bringing his shirt with her, and he made quick work of removing it and tossing it on the floor.

Karen wiggled her hips down, and she kissed his neck and chest down to his treasure trail. If she wasn't careful, he was worried he would explode right there.

"Oh, no, my sweet," he hissed to control his raging lust. "You need to behave. Wait, no...I can't believe I said that."

"Me neither," she said, and she continued kissing him.

From a faraway place he thought he heard his name, followed by a few loud bangs.

"Mr. St. Clare?"

Leo grabbed Karen's arms to still her.

"Mr. St. Clare, your room is ready."

"Thank you, Walter. Can you give us a few minutes and we'll meet you in the foyer?"

"Certainly."

Karen stood and tugged her dress down her hips. "Do you think he saw us?"

Leo sat up. "No. But I do believe he knew to stay out of sight."

After donning his shirt, Leo went to the table and picked up their wine glasses. Karen grabbed the wine bottle then turned to place a lingering kiss on his lips. "We won't need those."

Leo almost choked on his moan. "Hurry," he growled.

Karen giggled and dashed out of the dining room, Leo close behind.

Chapter 8

The smell of fresh coffee stirred Karen from a deep sleep. An odd quietness surrounded her, and she sat up with a start. It took a moment for her to remember she wasn't in her own bed...or the city. Following this revelation came a rush of other thoughts, both frustrating and erotic. *Who but Leo could evoke such a combination?*

Karen reached out to hold him, to make sure the night before hadn't been a dream, but his side of the bed was empty. Not again...

"Leo?" She recognized the panic in her voice and forced a deep breath. This was not like last time.

The buzzing in her ears stopped, and she heard whistling and the relaxing sound of water running from the master bedroom en suite. Relief settled her queasy stomach and she sighed.

So, it still bothered her after all this time. Here she'd hoped she'd grown up some. Pushing the covers off her, she grabbed an afghan from the foot of the bed and wrapped it around herself as she walked to the window. She pulled back the curtain and groaned at the sight of the winter wonderland outside. Her shoulder muscles tensed, and the pain radiated to her neck. She turned her head from side to side to stretch out the knots. No sense worrying about Natasha and her job. This circumstance was out of her control, and if Natasha couldn't see that then she'd be losing a great assistant. Karen saw her attempt at looking confident in the window's reflection and frowned. Oh, who was she kidding? Natasha probably had a happy dance choreographed and ready to go, but not without one last coffee run request.

Turning away from the window, Karen debated crawling back under the warm duvet and waiting for Leo to join her. Unfortunately, nature's call urged her into the washroom.

Leo peeked around the shower curtain when she entered and smiled. His gaze focused on her breasts. "Morning."

"Morning. I need to use the toilet."

Leo disappeared behind the shower curtain. "Don't let me stop you."

When had she become so comfortable with this man, she could go to the washroom with him in the room? After all the things they had done the night before was when. Karen's cheeks burned remembering what they had done with the wine.

He'd kept her up most of the night as they'd rediscovered each other, and it was better than she'd ever dreamed. He'd whispered Italian love words in her ear, but her favourite moment was the one in which he'd said, "My love." It had struck a chord even though she hadn't realised it at the time. What they had yet to discuss was the bone-melting kiss in the restaurant had been from Leo.

"Are you joining me any time soon?" Leo called from the other side of the curtain.

Karen shook off the bit of joy and confusion which had settled in her belly and flushed the toilet. Leo's shrieks were music to her ears as she joined him.

»»·««

"How much time do you need to get ready?" Leo asked as he towel-dried his hair after their extra-long session of lovemaking in the shower.

"Not too long. I need to ask Bea if she has a blow dryer."

"Okay, good. I'll go find Walter and get a few more details worked out."

"Are you going on a tour of the vineyard?"

"I doubt it." He pulled the curtain back and looked outside. "It may be sunny, but there's a lot of snow."

Karen joined him at the window. "Are we going to be able to get your car out of here?"

The scent of Dove soap from her skin invaded his senses, along with a hint of mint. If he didn't watch it, he'd have her naked and back in bed.

Leo stepped away to help clear his head. "Walter already offered to pull us to the main road."

Karen turned to face him, a small frown on her face. "Really?"

"We could stay here another night," he suggested.

Her hesitation gave him a bit of hope, but then she sighed and shook her head. "We can't."

And there it was—back to reality.

"Another time then?"

"Perhaps."

Leo watched as the look in her eyes turned wary. She didn't trust him, and he still didn't know how to open up. With her or his family. The protective armour was always on. How did you fix something or someone so broken? Leo let that question linger in his head for a minute before concentrating on more important things—like getting his Porsche back to New York in one piece.

He placed a chaste kiss on Karen's cheek and left the room.

His search for Walter ended quickly as he found him behind the front desk assisting another couple. Zipping up his coat, Leo went outside to find his car free of snow and a plowed path leading into the treed archway.

He unlocked the car door, sat behind the steering wheel, and turned the key in the ignition. The engine roared to life. He could always rely on his metal baby to behave. Unlike a certain woman inside the warm and cosy B&B. Last night she had been all fire and passion, a dream come true. Hell, thinking about their shower earlier this morning had him hard and aching. Then she had done a one-eighty and *pow*— she was a woman he didn't recognize. A woman who lacked confidence in her job, her ability to lead, and her talent for design.

But even more irksome was the thought of Karen with Paul. And if he wasn't careful, Leo would push her right into his arms.

He turned off the engine and headed back to the foyer, where Walter sat waiting for him. He placed his hopes on shop talk to cure his troubled thoughts as he followed Walter back outside.

»»·««

The enticing aroma of homemade bread filled Karen's nostrils as she strolled into the kitchen. Bea stood at the counter forming buns and humming a tune which reminded Karen of a lullaby.

"Good morning, Bea."

"Ah, there you are. How did you sleep?"

Karen's cheeks burned under Bea's scrutiny. "Umm, good."

"I think not. You didn't sleep." Bea winked at her and returned her concentration to the dough.

Karen's mind raced. Had they been loud the night before? Had the other guests complained? *OMG.*

"Bea, if we disturbed anyone—"

"Don't be silly," Bea scolded. She put the last bun in the pan beside her, laid a towel on top, and then placed the pan on the table in a ray of sunshine to rise. "Now come wash up and knead this for me. My hands aren't what they used to be."

Karen did as she was told. She sprinkled some flour on the dough and powdered her hands then started working the dough—out, over, in, flip. The repetitive movements were relaxing, and soon her tense shoulder muscles loosened.

Being in the kitchen cooking brought back wonderful memories of when Anna and her aunt and uncle lived with her. One year ago, Anna's uncle had up and sold his house without warning leaving them homeless, and Karen had invited them into her home. She'd loved having them there. People to care for and to have conversations with, other than her cat, Charlie. Having lost her parents to a car crash when she was eighteen, Karen cherished families still together. Perhaps if she hadn't been an only child...

Which was why Leo's attitude toward his family drove her crazy. Didn't he know how lucky he was to have people who loved him, people to joke and laugh with, fight with, rely on...unconditionally?

But she knew most families didn't fit the happily-ever-after mold.

"Karen, dear. You're beating up the poor dough."

Bea's voice cut through her thoughts. Karen groaned, put her hands up, and stepped back from the counter.

"Sorry."

"You're sorry for many things."

Karen wanted to blame it on her Canadian roots but bit her tongue. "Apparently so."

"Is it about your man, Leo?"

"Oh, he's not my man." Karen avoided Bea's glare as she pulled leftover dough off her hands.

"You are a smart woman?"

Karen lifted her chin and met Bea's gaze. "I like to think so."

"Then you're short-sighted."

"Well, yes, I do wear glasses when I have detailed seamstress work to do, but—"

"You love him."

Karen's mouth dropped open. A deafening silence filled the kitchen. Only after a minute could she hear a clock ticking in the other room. A rush of heat flowed from her head to her toes, and then her cheeks turned icy. She thought she might faint. "I...no."

"Ha. You young know nothing."

"I think I would know if I was in love." Karen said. Bea grunted and took over kneading the dough. "And no disrespect, but you don't even know me. This is the first time we've spoken since we arrived yesterday."

Bea kept her head down and her hands busy. "You are scared."

Karen stared at Bea. She wasn't scared—she was terrified. All her bravado of a moment ago vanished, and she bowed her head. "How do you...? I don't understand."

Her stomach swirled with anxiety, and the urge to shout overwhelmed her.

Bea wiped her hands on the towel she'd flung over her shoulder and made her way over to Karen. She took her hands and squeezed, the warmth like a soothing balm.

"I have been around for a long, long time, Miss Karen. Young couples, old couples...so much alike when they come to visit our B&B."

Karen looked into Bea's eyes, and the wisdom she saw in them awed her.

Bea led her to the window nook, and they sat. "There is false love. Hateful looks and words meant to hurt and belittle the other. Then we have one-sided love, where usually the man goes out of his way to impress the woman and gets nothing back."

Reclining against the window, Karen tucked her leg under her bum and relaxed. Bea's voice took on a hypnotic tone which eased the anxiety building up in Karen's stomach.

"We must not forget the lovey-dovey lovers who make you want to gag."

Karen laughed. "Definitely not."

"Another form of false love. It may seem cute in the eyes of the public, but once they get home it is a poisoned love doomed to fail, because there is no communication, lots of secrets, and no common ground.

"And then we have real love. These couples fight, laugh, talk, care, kiss, and when the other is not looking, they are smitten. You and Leo have real love. I can feel it down to my bones."

Karen shook her head. "We are experts at fighting."

"Good."

"There hasn't been much laughing this past week."

"But there has been some?"

"Yes," Karen agreed as the week reeled through her mind.

"And you have good talks, yes?"

A sarcastic laugh left her lips. "No, we don't. I try, I really do, but he always changes the subject."

"What do you ask him about?"

This woman had no shame, Karen realised. And for some reason, neither did she. "Well...why he left me without a word five years ago."

"Hmm, I would want an answer too."

"See. I'm not being unreasonable."

"But do you want this answer?"

Karen caught herself before shouting out a whole-hearted yes. Hadn't she been telling herself lately it didn't matter anymore after all these years?

"My head says it doesn't matter, but he broke my heart—and my heart wants to know."

"The heart sometimes wants what it doesn't need."

More words of wisdom, and how true they were, Karen thought.

"He has a secret. A big one he's not willing to share, even after all this time. How am I supposed to trust him?"

"Secrets are not wise."

"I know. What could possibly be so bad he doesn't think I'd understand? Unless he killed someone, he really has nothing to worry about."

The front desk bell rang, and Bea dashed out of the room. She sure could move fast for a lady in her seventies, Karen thought.

Karen walked back to the kitchen island and tried her hand at forming buns. She filled the baking pan and placed it with the others to rise. Hers were smaller, but she hoped Bea wouldn't mind.

Leo and Walter returned as she was kneading the remaining dough for the last batch.

"How did it go?" Karen asked as she brushed flour off the front of her dress.

"Really well. There's way more to this property than I imagined." Leo paused for a moment. "And you've taken a new post as kitchen assistant, I see."

Karen could picture the smirk on his face, but she refused to look. "Bea entrusted me with her special bun-forming technique...and she's a way better boss."

Leo grinned. "How hard will it be to tear you away from all this?"

Karen hesitated long enough to see Leo's brow crease in worry. "I'm in no hurry to get back."

"I know, but..."

"You will stay for lunch, then you can go." Bea rushed back into the kitchen and took Karen's post. "Go wash up," she added, and with expert precision she had the rest of the buns ready to go in record time.

With no more time to talk about what awaited them when they returned to Vale Designs, Karen and Leo pitched in to prepare a simple meal of fresh buns, cold cuts, cheese and pickles, and wine. Conversation centred around the property, with questions and observations Leo had regarding the vineyard.

Karen couldn't help but notice how excited Leo sounded. He'd borrowed her notebook and started taking his own notes and doodling images she didn't recognize of the yard.

If only he could see past the issues he had with his family and embrace what he was so obviously good at.

He even had Walter and Bea excited about the future prospects.

And maybe, just maybe, he'd stay in New York.

But would she? It really depended on Natasha's wrath. Even if Natasha didn't fire her, could she live with the daily tirades which would be so much worse?

Perhaps a new job search was in order. Something a little more prestigious than assistant. She took a long sip of her wine and pictured the gown on her dress form in her room. It was almost complete, and she itched to be home to apply the finishes Anna had suggested. She'd sent her pictures before leaving on her Valentine's date, and Anna had replied right away. Anna's excitement over the project had boosted Karen's much-needed confidence, and thoughts of wanting more out of a job than fetching coffee for the evil witch of New York bloomed.

After the meal, Bea put Karen and Leo to work at the sink washing and drying the dishes as she packed a basket of buns and homemade strawberry jam for them to take home. The normalcy of this household chore gave the moment an intimacy she didn't think possible, and a small spark of excitement took hold. Her feelings for Leo were more than an infatuation with their past relationship. She loved the man he was today. Karen's heart raced as she glanced over at Leo, who turned to grab more dirty dishes from the counter. Fear soon replaced excitement as she thought about the secret he kept from her. Feeling a bit woozy, she grabbed onto the sink's edge to steady herself.

He's leaving in a few days, her subconscious warned. *Then what?* Real love and secrets didn't mix, no matter how much she wanted Bea to be right.

Half an hour later, with chores complete and basket in hand, Karen embraced Bea in a tight hug. "I've known you for less than twenty-four hours and I'm sad to be leaving."

"Be strong and patient. Your man will smarten up soon," Bea whispered near her ear.

Karen pulled away. "How do you…?"

Bea touched her heart and Karen smiled. Oh, how she wanted to believe her. "Thank you."

Walter, with his tractor, guided them to the highway. All the snow had melted into slush puddles scattered across the road. With conversation at a minimum, Karen kept her eyes on the road and the music low so Leo could concentrate. It took an extra hour to reach the city, and with each passing minute her anxiety increased.

Leo was unable to find a parking spot anywhere in the vicinity of the office building, so Karen asked to be dropped off out front.

"I'll find a spot and meet you up there. Don't do anything stupid," Leo advised before pulling away from the curb.

"Thanks for the words of encouragement," Karen said. She faced the door, took a deep breath, and with head held high, marched inside and into the elevator.

»»·««

Leo had to park five blocks away. "This is why I have a chauffeur," he said to himself as he flipped his coat collar up to ward off the biting wind. Out at Bea and Walter's it'd been calm and sunny. Back in the city, snow had started falling again and the sky was grey and gloomy. From clouds or smog, he couldn't tell.

As he trudged down the slush-covered sidewalk, his cell phone rang. Leo glanced at the screen, which flashed a picture of his dad, and he pressed the talk button.

"Hey, Dad."

"Did you get a chance to look at the property in Hudson Valley?" Yep, Leo got his bad phone manners from his father.

"It's a B&B, Dad. A real gem."

His father sighed. "We don't have time to invest in a B&B, Leo, let alone learn anything about running one."

"They have a vineyard."

"Oh, good. What are the specs?"

"About five acres."

"Tiny—"

"Good crop, and the wine is delicious," Leo interjected.

His father grunted. "Not worth our time. I'll tell your mother."

"Dad?" Leo spoke into the phone, but there was only silence. He ended the call, tucked the phone into his jacket pocket, and swore.

His father may have well said, "You're not worth our time."

Damn him. What had gotten his goat anyway? Leo wondered. In all honesty, his father was usually the most pleasant one in the family. *Did the meetings in France not go well? Did he and Mom get into a fight?* They had at least three big fights throughout the year. It was February. *Valentine's Day?* Nah, his mother didn't care about such frivolous retail money grab days.

No anniversaries to forget. Birthdays…

Yes…a specific birthday. Leo stopped on the spot as his heart raced, and an instant headache pounded on his temples.

Today was his sister's birthday—would have been her birthday.

Leo's mind started to race. How could he possibly have forgotten? The surrounding buildings seemed to close in around him and his breathing became laboured. He needed to get out of there. He spun around and headed back to his car as flashes of his sister, Emily, popped in his head. A swimming pool, Emily laughing...then silence. He'd jumped into the water and grabbed her, but he was too late. She was dead.

Leo broke out in a cold sweat. Where the hell was his car? He ran a block, then two, and finally found his car parked outside a rundown pub. He took in his surroundings and noticed most of the neighbouring buildings matched the look of the pub. Situated behind a greasy and dusty solitary window was a flashing red "Open" sign. Feeling reckless and thirsty, Leo went inside.

The interior showed no better than the outside. It was dark and dingy; a single light bulb hung above the only pool table, and the area behind the bar was lit by cheesy fluorescent signs depicting naked women. The overwhelming scent of stale beer assaulted his nostrils.

A burly man with a full beard, shiny bald head, and tattooed arms stood behind the counter organising bottles.

"What can I get ya?" the man said without a glance in Leo's direction.

He shouldn't be there. Hell, he shouldn't be in New York. He should be home paying his respects at his sister's grave.

"Ya going to decide or what?" The bartender's growl was much louder now Leo had his attention.

"Scotch on the rocks." Decision made, Leo sat on the stool across from the bartender and slowly massaged his temples. The place matched his mood—dark and dangerous. "Leave the bottle."

»»•««

The elevator opened, and Karen stepped into the Vale Designs foyer. It was four o'clock in the afternoon and business as usual from what she could see. She didn't want anyone to see her and she sure as hell didn't want to talk to anyone, so instead of going to her desk, as would be her norm, she headed straight to Natasha's office.

After knocking twice, Karen opened the door. Natasha was sitting at her desk, phone to her ear, chewing on a pencil end. Once Karen was spotted, Natasha hung up on whoever was babbling in her ear and placed the pencil gently on the desk.

"Do you know what day it is?" Natasha asked as she stood and rounded her desk.

"What?" Karen bristled at the question but kept calm.

"Do you know what day it is?" Natasha repeated.

"Thursday," Karen enunciated slowly.

"Do you work on Thursdays?" Natasha sat on the corner of her desk and folded her hands in her lap.

"Yes."

"Were you at work today?"

Oh, this is ridiculous. "You know I wasn't at work today." So much for keeping her cool.

"And yesterday, where were you then?"

"On a photo shoot with Leo—"

"On a photo shoot, my ass." Natasha rose and crossed the span between them in three long strides.

"You okayed it."

"I didn't know—"

"You know all the goings on here."

Natasha said nothing, her gaze drawn to the door. "Where is Leo, by the way? I thought he'd be here to back you up."

Good question. He knew how much she needed him. "He's on his way up. He went to park the car."

"His Porsche?"

Karen frowned. "Yes."

"Love that car." Natasha returned to her chair. "I'm surprised he has it out in this weather." Her concern sounded syrupy and fake.

"It wasn't ideal. It took an extra hour to get back to the city."

Natasha's eyes narrowed in suspicion. "I didn't approve an out-of-town photo shoot, especially in the middle of winter."

Karen winced at her error. "I'm sure Leo didn't go behind your back and book something on his own." *Or did he?*

"I wouldn't put it past him...or you."

"Me? I did nothing but go on this assignment with your blessing. I can't control the weather or the unfortunate means of transportation."

"I needed you here."

For what? Her daily coffee run? "I tried—"

"I doubt it." Natasha flicked her hand in dismissal.

Something snapped in Karen's head. *Flick your hand again.*

Natasha stood, her gaze never leaving Karen, and flicked her hand so hard and fast her wrist cracked. Karen's eyes widened in surprise, while Natasha's mocked her.

"You were never good at keeping your thoughts to yourself."

"And you were never good at being nice."

She'd overstepped her bounds. Natasha's eyes closed to mere slits and her mouth pulled into a tight line.

"You're the worst assistant ever," Natasha spat back.

"And you are the world's worst boss." Karen couldn't keep her true thoughts from stumbling out her mouth.

Why were they doing this? Acting like a couple of spoiled brats in a who-could-say-the-meanest-thing-ever contest.

Catching her off guard, Natasha jabbed her finger into Karen's chest and pushed as hard as she could. Karen grabbed onto Natasha's arm to keep from falling back.

"I hate you." Natasha's voice was eerily calm.

"The feeling is mutual." Karen sneered.

They stood facing each other, neither backing down. After a few minutes of silence, Natasha's harsh demeanour returned, and she forced out a sarcastic laugh.

"I have no idea why Leo wastes his time with you," Natasha said.

Karen loosened her grip on Natasha's arm and sat on the couch. Her heart was like a heavy weight in her chest. She'd so often asked herself the same question.

"Look, Leo has nothing to do with this—"

"Yes, he does." Natasha smoothed out her long locks and stood. "You may think because you were stranded with him overnight you guys are an item now. Well, you can forget it. He's not relationship material. He's haunted.

Haunted? "Trying to scare me away so you can continue pursuing him by flaunting yourself like a show horse?"

A prickling of doubt crept into her heart as Natasha's smile widened.

"Oh, I'll always have a special place in Leo's heart. Unlike you. You're a passing fancy. Someone to keep him entertained while he's away from home."

"We're old friends," Karen said, but she knew how weak her words sounded.

"Old friends, hey? You know about his sister then?"

His sister? "Umm..."

Natasha laughed at her shaky attempt at confidence. "Apparently not."

"You'll say anything to hurt me. You've made it your number one mission since I arrived here."

"I'm trying to toughen you up. The fashion world is cutthroat."

"You treat no one else at Vale Designs with such disrespect." Karen's chest ached where Natasha poked her, and her heart felt bruised. "And I've had enough."

Natasha's surprise should have had Karen floating around the room in elation, but her lack of sleep the night before, the nerve-wracking drive back to the city, and their physical confrontation left her drained. To top it off, it appeared Leo had left her hanging again. All his promises of being around for her were empty puffs of smoke.

Maybe Natasha was right. She'd hoped after spending the night reconnecting with Leo that he'd changed. Foolish thought.

And what about his sister? He'd never mentioned her before. To be honest, Karen hadn't even known he had a sister.

"Tell me about Leo's sister."

Natasha sighed and started pacing the space between the couch and her desk. "It's not really my story to tell…"

Frustration rose in Karen's chest, pushing down the hurt. "Why did you mention her in the first place then?"

"Because..." Natasha stopped in front of Karen and wrapped her arms around her midsection. "I can see how much you adore him, and it's all an illusion."

"But you love him?"

"No."

"Oh, come on."

"I used to...when we were teenagers."

Right. Karen remembered Leo telling her about their high school friendship when they were in the women's washroom the other day—after the whole stealing-last-year's-design fiasco. An old friendship would explain why they were so at ease with each other. She envied that.

"He's always been the one who got away, but I've settled for what we have now." Back in her chair, Natasha spun around to face the windows.

Settled? Did romantic emotions still linger for her? It made sense now why Natasha wanted to sabotage any plans Karen had for a relationship with Leo. Did Leo know how unhealthy Natasha's feelings were?

"How's mentioning Leo's sister going to pop my illusions?"

Natasha stood and walked over to the windows. A mild smirk played at the corners of her mouth. "She's his ghost."

Karen paled and a chill ran up her spine. *His ghost?* "She's dead?"

"Yes. She's been dead for ten years." A low voice rumbled behind her.

Karen jumped off the couch and turned to see Leo standing in the doorway. She wanted to berate him for taking so long, but then she noticed how his posture was slouched and how his hair looked messy from the wind...or from running his hands through it one too many times. Something was wrong.

"Leo?" Karen walked slowly toward him, afraid to scare him off.

"Emily is dead," Leo blurted out. He tried to stand up straight, but he fell back against the doorframe.

"Are you drunk?" Anger ripped through Karen like nothing she'd ever experienced. He'd gone to a bar to get drunk instead of being by her side.

Leo hiccupped. "You bet."

Karen grabbed her purse and coat. A raging storm swirled inside her at the betrayal, but disappointment sat like a boulder on her heart. Tears welled in her eyes, but she refused to let them fall. When she spoke, it was barely more than a whisper.

"I'm done—with both of you." She turned to Natasha. "I quit."

Then she turned back to Leo and swallowed the huge lump of emotion caught in her throat. "I never want to see you again."

And she walked out without a second glance.

Chapter 9

Leo popped two extra-strength ibuprofens and downed the glass of water Robert handed him. His head pounded like a jackhammer against each temple, making him nauseous.

If Robert hadn't pinged his phone and found him in the rundown bar halfway into a terrible bottle of scotch, Leo would have been in way worse shape.

Now, looking out his living room window at the glistening streetlights below, he could feel the judgement in Robert's stare.

"Is there anything else you need before I retire for the night, sir?"

Leo knew if there was anything else, he wouldn't dare speak it. "No, I'm good. Thank you."

Robert nodded and gathered his coat. "I will see you in the morning then."

Leo nodded, not taking his eyes off his reflection in the window. The afternoon played through his mind like an old movie reel. Robert had swooped in on him and grabbed the bottle out of his hand which Leo tried to wrestle away, to no avail. Then the bartender had helped Robert get him into the limo, where Robert refused to talk to him after he asked where Karen had gone.

Leo had insisted he go up to Nat's office alone when they'd pulled up in front of Vale Designs. He didn't remember the elevator ride, but he did remember seeing Karen in her wrinkled sweater dress and dishevelled hair, and he couldn't remember when she'd looked more beautiful.

The room had started swaying, so he'd hitched a hip against the doorframe until things had steadied, but then he'd heard Karen ask Nat about his sister. His stability had crashed to the floor and he'd blurted out his response. For as long as he lived, he'd remember the look on Karen's face before she walked out of the room.

He hadn't stayed to talk to Nat, but somehow, he'd made it back to Robert, who had been standing inside the foyer with his arm proffered to guide him back to the limo.

How he wanted to sleep...hell, he hadn't gotten a lot the night before, either. Thoughts of Karen naked and moving above him had his cheeks flushed. He pressed the water glass to each cheek and turned away from the panoramic view.

With a heavy sigh, Leo sat in his favourite reclining chair, reached for a remote, and clicked on the fireplace. Warmth soon filled the room, along with his tired and weary body. Closing his eyes, he expected to see more images of Karen, but his mind was blank, and he fell asleep in moments...only to have his slumber broken by persistent knocking.

"Hold on," he barked, and he slowly made his way to the door.

"Did you forget your key?" He opened the door expecting to see Robert but instead found Natasha, all bombshell knockout, smiling up at him.

She trailed her hand down his chest. "You never did give me a key."

Leo knocked Natasha's hand away. "I thought you were Robert."

"I definitely am not." She paused. "Can I come in?" Leo stepped aside so she could pass. "I forgot what this place looked like. It's been a while since you've had me over." She peeled off her gloves and dropped them on the table, followed by her scarf and coat.

"I have a bench in the foyer for all your stuff, Nat."

"Yes, yes." She flicked her hand in dismissal and made her way to the wet bar. "What does a girl have to do to get a drink around here?"

Leo returned from dumping her stuff on the floor by the front door. "What would you like?"

"Gin and tonic."

Her drink of choice. "Coming up. Why don't you sit down?"

Nat grabbed a blanket from the back of the couch and curled up in the corner closest to the fireplace. Leo watched her tuck her legs under the blanket and wished with all his might Karen was the one making herself comfortable on his couch, in his home, and in his bed. Why had he never had her over to see his place before?

Because he brought all his one-night stands here, and Karen wasn't either of those things. He enjoyed her company, and she made him laugh. She genuinely cared about other people, and five years ago she'd cared about him enough to seek out a friendship. Unfortunately, his guilt had outplayed him, stopping him from getting close to anyone back then, his secret uppermost in his mind...always. It controlled his life even now and had ruined any second chance of a future with Karen.

"So, to what do I owe the pleasure of your company?" Leo asked as he handed over her cocktail.

"You didn't stay to chat after Kara left."

"It's Karen, Nat...and I was in no mood to chat."

She sipped her drink and then smiled. "Perfect as always."

Wide-awake now and his headache only a numb throbbing, Leo paced the space behind the couch. "And we have nothing to talk about."

Natasha let out a dramatic sigh before taking another sip of her drink.

He'd let Karen down. She'd needed him during what she knew was going to be a terrible ordeal. And what had he done? He'd reverted to his old ways and panicked over the past, got drunk, and made a fool of himself. Same old Leo.

Karen was one of the strongest people he knew. His rock. Now it was his turn to be hers. No more living in the past.

"Why are you staring at me like that?" Nat asked.

Leo ran his hand through his hair and down his neck. "You were discussing my sister with Karen."

"Well, yes, but—" Nat stammered.

"No one talks about my sister but me."

"Yes, I remember you mentioning it before, but—"

"No one." He shouted.

"She said she knew." Natasha shouted back at him.

"And you believed her?"

"Why wouldn't I?" Her eyes darted to the window and back to him. The fear was gone, replaced by cocky confidence. Was this a vindictive act against him and Karen for getting stuck at the B&B overnight?

Leo could feel his second wind draining, but his thoughts of Karen kept him going.

"Can I make you a drink?" Natasha stood beside him now and whispered in his ear.

Leo grasped her wrist and pushed her away. "Get out."

"What?"

"You betrayed my trust and hurt my...Karen. I want you to leave. Now."

Natasha's fake hurtful expression magically turned into her famous Wicked-Witch-of-the-West grin. "You are under contract, and I expect—"

"I will finish out my contract with you, and you'll be loved and envied by all. When this Fashion Hell Week is over, so are we."

»»·««

Karen pulled back the lapel and pinned it in place. Stepping back, she took in the almost complete look of her newest creation. Anna had been right. Adding the white stripe in the collar and lapel had given the tuxedo dress a sophisticated and feminine look.

Sneaking a peek at the clock on her bedside table, she saw it was midnight. She'd worked nonstop since arriving home, taking no breaks to eat and only having the occasional sip of wine, and time had flown by. Half an hour later, she tied off the stitch she was working on. All she had left to do was attach the cufflinks.

Her heart filled with joy and pride.

Then her brain said, "Now what?"

Karen closed her eyes to stop the tears from falling and then exhaled deeply as they escaped and rolled down her cheeks.

The events of the afternoon were now a blur, but she wished her heart would stop hurting. The ache was deep and consumed her chest and throat so all she wanted to do was cry. Working on the dress had taken all her concentration, and she'd reveled in the long break from overthinking what happened in Natasha's office.

Desperate to talk to someone, Karen picked up her cell phone and punched in Anna's phone number. It was only nine thirty in Vancouver.

"Hello?"

"Hi, Anna." Her voice quivered with emotion.

"Karen. What's wrong?"

Crying and babbling nonsensical words, she paced her bedroom and gestured wildly as if Anna could see her frustration and pain.

"I'd be there for you in a second if I wasn't thirty-six weeks pregnant," Anna blurted out when Karen finally stopped ranting.

"I know." Now all her concerns and fears were out in the open, all her pent-up energy seeped from her body, leaving her tired and weak. "I could really use one of your hugs."

"What if I send Jace in my place?"

Karen smiled. "As nice as it would be to see him, he's not you."

"I am irreplaceable."

Karen chuckled, easing a bit of the ache around her heart. "Definitely."

A comfortable silence filled the air between them, but Karen had to ask, "You're not mad I quit and lost our ticket into the fashion scene?"

"Not at all. There are plenty of other experts we can approach."

"Not in New York…"

"What do you mean?"

"Natasha is a nasty witch who will make sure I never get another job in this city."

"Umm, are you sure you aren't—?"

"I'm not overreacting. Trust me."

"Okay."

The silence this time was tense, but Karen could picture the wheels turning in Anna's head.

"Do you think you'll be able to get into the closing gala?"

Karen grunted. "Not bloody likely." Well, there could be a way in…if she asked Leo to take her which meant seeing him again, and her parting words had suggested otherwise. "Why?"

"I have a plan for your dress."

"Do tell."

The muffled sound of a door slamming had Karen turning around in surprise. "Someone's here."

"Don't hang up until you tell me who it is," Anna said.

"Karen, you home?" a male voice shouted.

Karen sighed with relief. "It's Mike. I'd better go and talk to him. He's probably freaked out because I didn't come home last night."

"As he should be. He's a good friend."

"Yes, he is."

"You still haven't told me what you're going to do about Leo," Anna said in a rush before Karen could end the call.

Karen closed her eyes as the familiar ache intensified. "I thought for a second maybe he'd changed, but he's an insensitive moron who thinks only of himself. He's never going to change, Anna, which makes me even more of a moron for still wanting him."

"You love him," Anna said.

Heaven help her, she did. "How can I love someone who keeps secrets, breaks promises, and won't grow up and take responsibility for anything?"

"Go and see him. Make him talk. Find out why—"

"I told him I never want to see him again."

"Which will show how much you care and will forgive."

Karen's stomach started a topsy-turvy dance making her nauseous. "I don't know if I can do that."

"Are you willing to live with a 'what if'?"

She headed downstairs to see Mike, pride hardening her heart. "Yes."

»»·««

The late morning sunshine warmed Leo's face as he adjusted his camera lens yet again. This photo shoot should be a simple thing. His crew had taken possession of a heavily treed corner in Central Park for the last shoot before Fashion Week wrapped up the following night with the closing gala. His mission today was to capture nature—the fresh pine scent of the Blue Atlas cedars, the crisp snow under foot, and the rosy-red cheeks of the model. Today, the model, Tanya, wore black leggings, tan boots, and a long red winter coat with a fur hood.

The colours complemented the soft green from the cedars, and the bright sunshine hinted at a warm winter wonderland, when in reality it was damn cold.

His fingertips were frozen, which made adjusting his camera nearly impossible. A few choice swear words flowed freely from his mouth as he stomped over to the propane fire pit one of the crew had set up to keep them warm. Rubbing his hands together, he placed them as close to the fire as he could and glanced around him. If Karen had been there, there wouldn't have been such chaos. True, nothing more serious than some mingling near the coffee station threatened the scene, but Leo had to admit he'd gotten used to Karen's way of handling a photo shoot. Her confident and caring nature had won everyone's hearts...except

Nat's. And after the day before, Karen wanted nothing more to do with him. Now that she had no job, she was probably on her way home to Vancouver.

Her last words to him rang through his head like a loud gong echoing off the walls, and a stab of guilt hit him hard and fast.

It was all due to a past which refused to stop haunting him. He had to figure out how to deal with Emily's death and why his family treated him like delicate china. But most importantly, it was time to grow up.

"Figured I'd be the one to say that to you."

Leo turned to find his brother, Luke, standing a few feet away. Far enough so Leo couldn't punch him. Typical.

And now he apparently had taken up Karen's bad habit of talking out loud.

"What are you doing here?"

"Glad to see you too."

A couple of the crew hanging around the fire took their cue and wandered over to the coffee station, giving them some privacy.

Leo stepped closer and embraced Luke in a bear hug. "It's good to see you."

"You as well." Luke tilted his head in recognition of the crew and the shoot set-up. "This suits you."

"Unlike the family business."

Luke turned to face the fire and warm his hands. "We've always wanted you involved with the wineries."

Leo sighed. He knew Luke spoke the truth. "Did Dad send you to check up on me?"

"He mentioned you were quite passionate about the little B&B and wanted to know why. So yes."

Leo stared into the fire, his lips forming a small smirk. "I got a whole other impression from my little chat with Dad."

"He had a hard day yesterday. We all did."

Leo ran his thumb and forefinger across his eyebrows to help relieve the tension headache he now had.

"I hated you guys for being gone all the time at one damn winery or another. Always leaving me and Emily alone..."

He heard Luke's deep intake of breath and continued. "First the divorce and then Emily's freak accident. I was eighteen years old and so frustrated having to be stuck babysitting all the time when my friends were out having the time of their lives."

"You never mentioned this before."

"You guys tiptoed around me and treated me like Grandma's delicate china." Leo's voice cracked. "It was my fault she drowned, Luke. Why won't you get angry with me, or hell, beat me up? I deserve no less." Leo looked up to see a few of the crew looking over at them. "Go for lunch, everyone," he called.

Once everyone had cleared out, Luke stepped away from the fire's heat. "You did everything you could to save her, and in our grief, we let you take full blame."

Leo could see the faraway look in Luke's eyes and knew he was remembering that day. But not Luke, nor their mom or dad, had been there when it had happened. None of them would be haunted by the blank stare of her lifeless eyes.

Instead of being resentful, as was his nature around his family, Leo felt grateful for his brother's presence and realised all four of them were mourning Emily in their own way. And after all this time, none of them had the closure they needed to move on.

"I think we need to see a counsellor."

Luke looked up at him, the blank stare disappearing to reveal hope. "You and me?"

"Yes. Mom and Dad too."

Luke reached in his coat pocket and pulled out a tissue to blow his nose. "This weather is atrocious. My nose hasn't stopped running since I got here."

"Nice cover, brother," Leo said with a grin.

"You've been dealing with this on your own for much too long," Luke said, ignoring Leo's jibe and standing a little closer to the fire.

Leo's grin disappeared as thoughts of Karen returned. "Yes, I have, which is my fault as well."

"You distanced yourself from everyone who cares about you."

"Yes." And Nat, the one person he had confided in all those years ago had betrayed his trust.

Karen would never do that. Not now or five years ago. Realisation dawned as a euphoric sensation took hold, and he knew his heart had always belonged to her.

"So how are we going to fix this?" Luke asked as he pulled a flask out of his pocket.

"Fireball?"

"None other." Luke twisted off the cap and took a long swig. "Your turn."

Leo took a smaller sip, still feeling the effects of the day before. "You sticking around for a day or two?"

"If you need me, I'll be here."

"You remember Karen Allen?"

Luke's eyes lit up. "The hottie from college you were 'friends' with?"

"Yes, and don't get any ideas."

"I would never—"

"Save it," Leo interrupted. "I hope you brought a tux. You're my date to the closing gala tomorrow night."

Leo would get Robert to stop Karen from leaving New York, and then he'd take care of the rest.

»»•««

The white frothy leaf floating on top of her latte disappeared as she stirred in a cube of sugar. Karen took the tiniest bit of pleasure sitting in the coffee shop she'd frequented so much when fetching Natasha her daily beverage.

"Hey, Ms. Allen. I got your text."

Karen smiled up at Kim as she sat down across from her.

"Do you want anything?"

"Coffee."

Karen raised her eyebrows in question, and Kim sighed. "Okay, okay. Tea, please."

Karen signalled a waitress and ordered then turned to Kim. "Have you spoken with Ms. Vale about your predicament?"

Kim shook her head and stared at the tabletop. "I'm sure she already knows."

"Most likely. Frequent vomiting for days on end is a hard thing to hide."

"I've never been so scared in all my life." A tear streaked down Kim's cheek, and she wiped it away before it fell to the table. Her tea arrived, and she took a small sip and then leaned back in her chair.

"Scared to tell Ms. Vale about the baby, or to bring a new life into this world all alone?"

"Two for two." Kim frowned and wiped away another tear.

"Have you seen a doctor?"

"No. It'll make all of this seem more real."

"Right."

"And I'm not ready to deal with real yet."

Karen closed her eyes and took a deep breath. Why did she seem drawn to the type of person who refused to grow up and accept responsibilities? Well, this time she refused to keep quiet.

"Welcome to the real world, Kim." With her tone a bit harsh, she had Kim's attention.

"What?"

"You're eighteen years old, I get it. But this is the life you chose, and you need to make a decision before it's too late."

Whatever was in Kim's tea had her mesmerised. "I don't know what to do."

"You need to answer some important questions."

"Like what?" Kim asked.

"Can you raise a baby in your current circumstances?"

"I'm sharing an apartment with three other models, so what do you think?"

Karen refused to take Kim's tone personally. "What will you do about childcare?"

"My career will be over once a baby bump starts to show."

"What about family? New York isn't home, is it?"

"I ran away from home to chase this dream. They won't take me back, let alone a baby."

She really did have quite a conundrum. "Then you have some serious soul searching to do. You either go home and raise this baby with your family's help or you have the baby and give it up for adoption. Mind you, you won't have the same body after going through a pregnancy and delivery."

Kim's eyes widened in alarm.

"Or you terminate the pregnancy and keep on with your glamorous career."

Kim gulped back the rest of her tea and made to stand, but Karen grabbed her hand. "I'm not trying to scare you, Kim. I'm trying to help."

"I'm more stressed out than I was before," Kim screeched, and people at the nearby tables stopped their conversations to stare.

"It's time to be an adult, Kim. You need to make a decision and stick with it. No one said it was going to be one iota of easy."

Kim flopped back into her chair. "This sucks."

Karen let out a small chuckle. "Yes, it does."

"I ruined everything."

"It may seem so right now."

Kim looked up into Karen's face, desperation in her eyes. "What would you do?"

"Well, I'm not a model, so I don't rely on my looks to succeed."

"Oh yeah…"

"Look, Kim. You're young and have your whole life ahead of you. You need to figure out if you want to raise a child right now or if you want to expand your career."

The two of them sat quietly for a long while until Kim broke the silence. "There are rumours going around that you quit."

Karen nodded with a smile. "I did, and it was one of the most terrifying things I've ever done. I've ruined my chances of getting a similar job in this city, and I've let down my partner back home. I have nothing left here."

Kim leaned forward on her elbows, her chin resting in her hands. "Wow. What will you do now?"

"Go back to Vancouver. Take some down time and then get back in the game."

"Sounds like we have more in common than I thought."

Karen finished her latte with a grimace. "Yeah."

"Thanks for talking to me, Ms. Allen, and giving me a few things to think about."

"I hope I helped a bit."

"You did." Kim stood and slipped her coat back on. "Wish me luck."

For both of us. Karen had a sudden thought. "Do you want to go out with a bang?"

Kim nodded her curiosity piqued.

"Come by my place tomorrow morning." Karen scribbled down her address on a napkin. "We can say farewell to Ms. Vale together."

»»·««

Big fluffy snowflakes fell in a lazy pattern, decorating the park like a scene from a fairy tale. Karen took her time walking down the path, smiling at people walking by with their dogs or humming along to the music playing in their ear buds. Finding a deserted bench, she sat and realised this was the first time since arriving in New York she wasn't running an errand, and the city didn't seem like a depressed and angry monster that never slept. Yes, the downtown core buzzed with never-ending energy, but when away from it all, a person could find some normalcy.

And time to think...about a certain man she'd banned from her life. Anna had asked her if she could live with the what-if of never seeing him again, never finding out the real reason behind his behaviour. Thanks to Natasha's indiscretion, she was sure it had something to do with his sister, but what damage her death had done she couldn't know. Karen had been adamant before ending the phone call she could live without knowing. Hadn't she gone this long already?

Their time at the B&B seemed like a dream now. She'd seen a side of him which had brought such joy and promise. When they'd reconnected sexually, she'd felt so alive, so young, and happy. And it was over as fast as it had begun.

What was the point of trying to get into his head again when she knew so well where the road led? It had been the same five years ago as it was today, and she didn't think her heart could take much more.

Her cell phone buzzed in her jacket pocket, startling her from her reflections. Karen pulled it out and frowned at the screen. A message from Paul. He wanted to meet. According to Mike, Paul had been worried about her, so she wasn't surprised to get the message. She wanted to be happy Paul was still interested in her, but her heart had no room for a new relationship right now.

But she did need to get into the closing gala, and Paul had revealed on their Valentine's date he had tickets—his cousin was one of the makeup artists. Now that he'd reached out, she knew she had her way in. She stomped down the growing guilt of having to use him and dialled his number.

"Hi, Paul."

"Hey. How are you? I've been worried sick."

"I had an out-of-town photo shoot and got stuck out there due to the storm with no cell service."

"Yeah, Mike told me."

Karen heard the doubt in Paul's voice and frowned. A good five-second silence passed before Karen said, "Paul? You still there?"

"Mike told me you thought I kissed you in the restaurant the other night..."

OMG. Heat filled her cheeks as she focused on a dog chasing a ball in the field across from her. The plan she'd had was going up in smoke. "Yes."

"Do you know who it was?"

"No." The lie rolled smoothly off her tongue.

"Really?" He did not sound convinced.

"I thought I had to keep the blindfold on until I was in the washroom..."

"And?"

"And I thought it was you." Karen's voice hitched in anger at his sarcastic tone.

A few seconds of tense silence passed. "Did you want it to be me?" Paul asked, his voice barely a whisper.

At the time, yes. "Maybe."

"Where does this leave us then?"

"Friends, I hope."

"As good a place as any, I suppose." Paul sighed.

Karen smiled. "Well then, friend. Do you need a date for the closing gala?"

"As a matter of fact, I do."

Her guilt dissipated a bit. Her plan was going to work after all.

»»·««

The next morning dawned bright but much too soon. Working on last-minute alterations had kept Karen up until three in the morning. She'd collapsed onto her bed fully clothed with enough energy to grab the edge of the blanket and pull it over herself before falling into a deep slumber.

Unsure what had woken her, since she hadn't set an alarm clock, Karen sat up and stretched. It took a bit longer for her brain to wake up, which was understandable since there was no morning coffee in her hand.

"I need coffee," she mumbled, and she rolled out of bed. Catching a glimpse of her reflection in the mirror, she gasped. Yesterday's clothes were wrinkly and hung on her frame. Her hair was a mess and her eye makeup was smeared down her cheeks.

"First I must remedy this." Karen took a detour to the shower and then slipped on her yoga pants and an old school sweater before heading down to the kitchen to start a pot of coffee. One day she was going to buy Mike a programmable coffeemaker so all they would have to do is pour and go.

Oh, right. There wouldn't be "one day" after she moved back to Vancouver. All the memories and emotions that had consumed her over the last two days filled her heart to aching. Try as she might to keep herself so busy, she'd run herself to exhaustion, the hurt still returned at the most inconvenient times.

Karen inhaled deeply as the coffee aroma filled the kitchen. She poured a liberal amount into her favourite cat mug and let the built-up tears fall down her cheeks. How was it possible a person could hurt this much without dying from heartache?

A loud wail escaped her and turned into a sob. Her hands shook so hard, she had to put the mug back on the counter. She slid down the cupboards and sat on the floor, knees to her chest, head on her knees and let all the pain rush out in her tears.

Maybe Anna had been right. She should go to Leo and demand his explanation for breaking her heart. But what if she didn't like his response? What if he didn't have one, other than his nonchalant shrug and cocky grin?

Tomorrow none of this would even matter to him. He was going to return to his estate in Tuscany, and this past week would only be a memory, their time together an extra notch on his bedpost. She'd return to Vancouver and lay low until another opportunity presented itself.

"Ugh, that sounds dreadful."

Karen lifted her head to find Mike standing in front of her.

"Hey. I suppose my breakdown woke you up."

"You could say that." He grabbed a mug from the cupboard and poured himself some coffee.

"Sorry," she said, and she wiped the tears from her face.

"You're not wasting tears on that evil witch boss of yours, I hope."

Karen stood and took hold of her mug. "Definitely not. Quitting that job was the best thing I've ever done."

"Agreed."

She took a sip of her lukewarm coffee then smiled. "I'm glad I woke you up."

Mike's eyebrows practically disappeared into his hairline. "Oh really?"

"Sleeping in is overrated."

"Only you would think that."

"Whatever you say, Mr. Lawyer Man."

"You know what you plan to do now?"

Karen knew he was referring to going back home to Vancouver. "What choice do I have? It'll be nearly impossible to get a job here with the kind of influence Natasha has in this town."

"You shouldn't underestimate your talent."

"Thanks, but—"

"I saw your dress."

Karen's eyes widened with surprise. "You were in my room?"

"Well, when I heard you crying, I rushed out to find you. Your bedroom was the first place I checked."

"Oh."

"To be honest, I have no idea why you're fetching coffee and trying to learn the ropes when you obviously know more than most of the people at Vale Designs."

Karen's eyes swelled with more tears. Apparently, her heart still had room for a tiny bit of pride.

"Thank you," she said.

The doorbell rang.

"Are you expecting someone?" Mike asked, heading out of the kitchen.

Karen followed Mike to the front door. Kim wasn't due to come over for another two hours yet. "Who is it?"

Mike turned around, carrying a huge parcel.

"It's for you. From someone named Leo."

Chapter 10

Karen took the box from Mike and headed to the living room, where she placed it on the coffee table.

"Who's Leo?" Mike asked joining her.

"An old friend."

What was Leo about, sending her a gift? She lifted the top and gasped. Inside lay the most stunning gown she'd ever seen. Karen lifted it out of the box and held it in front of her.

Mike gave a low whistle of approval. "He's some old friend."

Karen ignored Mike and held the gown to her body. The silver satin bodice was strapless and form-fitting to the waist. The silvery fabric continued down the back and sides over black gossamer that peek-a-booed at the front and was tied together in front of the left hip with a black-gemmed flower brooch.

She handed the dress to Mike and turned her attention back to the box. Inside she found a pair of silver heels, a jewellery box, and an envelope. Karen's heart was racing so fast she thought she might faint. Sitting on the couch, she placed the jewellery box on her lap and opened it slowly. Nestled inside lay three tear-shaped amethyst diamonds, so dark they appeared black, hanging on a delicate silver chain. Karen's mind went numb as she stroked the stones.

"Holy crap." Mike chimed in.

"I don't understand," Karen said, shaking her head.

"Open the envelope."

"Okay." Her hands shook as she peeled back the top of the envelope and pulled out the letter.

An invitation to the closing gala and award show. On the bottom in Leo's scrawl were the words, *Please come. I'll be looking for you.*

Karen tossed the invitation back into the box, closed the jewellery box, and placed it inside as well. Standing, she held out her hands for the dress.

"What are you doing?" Mike asked, hugging the dress closer to his body.

"Is this his idea of an apology? He can't buy me back with gorgeous and outrageously expensive presents."

"He can't?"

"No, he can't." Karen wanted to be mad, but with Mike standing there hugging the ball gown like a lost lover, she couldn't work up the energy.

"Sometimes this is how men apologise, since opening our big mouths even more can be disastrous."

"Sometimes women need to hear the words and see the struggle. It means more to us than any fancy gift."

"You're one-of-a-kind, Karen. No one I've ever gone out with thinks like that."

Karen smirked. "That's because you don't date women."

"That's true."

The doorbell rang again, and Karen ran to answer it this time. She flung the door open, but no one was there. Another box with a single red rose lay on the welcome mat. She scooped it up and returned to the living room.

"Another gift?" Mike asked. He hung the dress over the back of the couch.

"Do you have a vase?"

"You're asking a bachelor if he has a vase?"

"What was I thinking?" Karen said with a smile. "What about a tall glass?"

"Tall glass I can do." Mike disappeared into the kitchen, and Karen sat on the couch and placed the new package on her lap.

Afraid she'd find another small fortune worth of jewels, she opened the box and found a framed photo of a young girl, maybe ten years old. A sense of knowing fluttered in her stomach, and her heart filled with something a bit different from heartache. Karen lifted the photograph out and took a closer look. The girl had the biggest smile on her face. She was jumping on a trampoline, mid-jump, with her long blond hair floating in a huge halo above her head.

"Who's that?" Mike asked, returning with a glass for the rose.

"I think it might be Leo's sister." Karen handed the picture to Mike and checked inside the box, where she found another envelope. Her hands shook as she peeled back the opening to reveal another note in Leo's handwriting. She read out loud to Mike. "'This is my sister, Emily. It's time for me to talk about her and the tragic loss of such a beautiful spirit. Please text a yes or no to Robert at the number below if you will be joining me at the gala. If yes, he will pick you up at nine thirty.'"

"Let me see if I've got this right," Mike said. "Leo is an old friend who spoiled you rotten with a Cinderella gown and jewels, and he wants to open up about his past. What kind of spell did you place over the poor guy?"

"Hell if I know." Karen sighed as she leaned back against the couch.

"So then, will it be yes or no?"

Karen stood in one graceful movement. "I don't know."

"For the love of Pete. The man is trying to make things better."

"I know, but—"

"But what?" Mike asked, and he threw his hands up in frustration.

"I'm already going with Paul."

"What?" Mike's hands hit his thighs with a thud.

"I extinguished any hope of going when I quit my job. I also told Leo I never wanted to see him again. I didn't have a lot of options."

"I guess not."

"We ended up talking about my mysterious kiss."

"Which I bet was actually Leo."

"How did you—? Ugh, it doesn't matter." Karen shook her head and shrugged. "Yes, it was Leo, but I didn't figure it out until the next day."

"You did appear quite distraught after the kiss happened."

"What should I do?" Karen buried her face in her hands.

"Paul's a good guy and a good friend of mine. He doesn't deserve to be used."

Karen dropped her hands and turned to face Mike. "I'm not using him, not anymore. We're going as friends."

"And he knows this?"

"Yes."

"But does he believe it?"

"I hope so." Karen averted her eyes at Mike's stern glare.

"Don't give him any false hope. You're going with Leo."

She nodded and busied herself putting the rose in the glass of water, the scent filling her nose. Part of her wanted to say no to Leo, show up with Paul, and say, "It's too late for any explanations now, buster," but could she really be that vindictive when he appeared to finally be reaching out to her? Did she want to hurt either of them to get herself into the gala?

No, she didn't. Yet could she sacrifice her heart one more time? Karen closed her eyes and sighed. Did she really have a choice?

"I'll call Paul."

"Thank you," Mike said.

Karen slipped her cell phone out of her secret yoga-pant pocket and entered Robert's number into her phone. She texted "yes" and then dialled Paul's number.

"Let me know when Kim gets here," Karen said to Mike as the phone rang in her ear. "Oh, and wish me luck." Karen headed upstairs to her room for some much-needed privacy.

»»•««

"You were right. This place is amazing."

Leo barely heard his brother. He was still reflecting on the text he'd received from Robert on the drive there. Karen had said yes. His body hummed with nervous energy. She was going. She was giving him another chance. He felt like a giddy teenager about to go on a first date with the head cheerleader.

"Earth to Leo." Luke tapped him on the shoulder.

"Sorry. What?"

"You okay?"

"Yeah... yes. My plan is falling into place."

"Good news then, right?"

Leo closed his eyes and focused on the twittering of the winter birds. "Why am I so nervous?"

"Because your girl has given you another chance and you're about to reveal your heart to her. The unknown is scary."

Leo looked at Luke with a newfound respect. "Listen to you, Mr. Romance."

Luke punched Leo in the shoulder. "Shut up."

"Touchy," Leo said, rubbing at the sore spot.

"So, now I have a visual, why don't you tell me about your plans for this place?" Luke said, changing the subject with his usual suaveness.

Leo noticed Walter making his way toward them and waved. "This is Walter, the best man for the job. He'll give you such a detailed tour you'll never want to leave."

"Exactly what I want to hear. Hello, Walter, I'm Luke, Leo's brother." He extended his hand in welcome.

"Ah, you are twins?" Walter asked, looking from one brother to the other.

Luke laughed. "We get that a lot, but no. I've got a good five years on him."

"Hey, you make it sound like I look old and you look young," Leo said.

"It is what it is, baby brother." Luke grinned and stepped out of the way of Leo's punch.

"Hmph."

"Come then," Walter said, turning away and heading to the vineyard.

Leo checked his watch. It was close to noon. Lots of time for a quick tour, the two-hour drive back to the city, and then the gala. Having Luke there to see what a gem the B&B was and to have his support was priceless. Imagining Karen in the gown he'd picked out for her and holding her in his arms again as they danced the night away made him giddy. So, this was what happiness felt like. It'd been so long, he'd practically forgotten. Everything was falling into place.

Walter didn't disappoint. After getting a thorough background on the vines, they headed inside for a tour of the house where Leo showed Luke his diagrams for the renovations. Bea made them a late lunch of Margherita pizza, and Walter paired it with the perfect dry rosé.

Happy and full, Leo and Luke said their goodbyes and got inside the Jeep 4x4 Luke had rented for his visit. A much better ride than Leo's Porsche in the winter weather.

A steady stream of jazz played on the radio as Leo professionally navigated the Jeep onto the highway.

The sun shone and there was barely a cloud in the sky, but the snow was still piled high in the ditches. He quickly glanced at the dashboard clock and saw it was four o'clock. Anxiety churned in his stomach. The tour and lunch had taken way longer than he'd thought. The drive itself took two hours if traffic was light, but with the start of rush hour, Leo had his doubts.

He put his foot on the clutch and shifted into fifth gear. The Jeep jerked forward as Leo sped up.

"Take it easy, leadfoot."

"We took longer than I planned. With rush hour, we'll be lucky to get back to the condo, change, and be at the gala before Karen gets there."

"Ah, yes, your grand plan."

Leo stole a quick look over at his brother. He didn't miss the sarcasm. "I can't screw this up."

"You don't think she'd understand?"

"I've hurt her so much. Her trust is like a spider web right now."

"A unique analogy. Why do you think Karen is so fragile?"

"I don't think—" Leo started to shout then took a deep breath and eased back on the gas pedal.

"You want everything to be perfect, but life isn't perfect."

"I know…"

"What I'm trying to say is the best plans are the ones unplanned."

Leo turned on the windshield wipers as a light rain began to fall. Luke had a good point. Used to solving problems and making friends with extravagant gifts, for Leo it was a no-brainer to do the same with Karen. But Karen was not in the same scope. She deserved so much better and a more personal approach. Yet he'd sent the picture of Emily after the gown and jewels, as if it were an afterthought.

He slammed his palm on the steering wheel. "What was I thinking?"

"A quick way to happily-ever-after is my first guess." Luke reached over to turn down the music.

Leo slapped Luke's hand. "No one touches the dials."

"This is my car, not yours," Luke argued back.

"I'm driving."

"I'm navigating."

Leo's thoughts drifted to a few days earlier, when Karen had navigated on their drive to the B&B. What a day. In his mind's eye, he pictured them holding hands and strolling up and down the vineyard rows on a hot summer day or sitting in front of a roaring fire with a glass of wine in the middle of a winter storm, cosy and safe in each other's arms. A future with Karen seemed within reach.

But a future with someone else had his stomach in knots. He'd always envisioned being a bachelor until his dying day. Racing cars and playing poker then retiring to restore old cars in the garage. As dull as that may have sounded to some people, that future gave him comfort.

Leo tightened his grip on the steering wheel and twisted his hands. The wailing sound of a trumpet solo from the jazz station had his heart pumping rapidly. Maybe this wasn't such a good idea. What did he know about real relationships anyway? He lived for life in the fast lane, sleeping in until noon, partying every night, and changing girlfriends at the first spark of boredom. He did what he wanted, when he wanted. Never needing anyone's permission or advice. This stint in New York was only a welcome break from the ordinary. He wasn't supposed to fall in love with Karen or a vineyard —but he'd gone and done both.

Panic set in good and deep. He glanced over at Luke, who was humming along to the melody of a peppy jazz tune. What would his brother say to him if he called it all off and went home, pride wounded but his heart still intact? His brother could have the B&B, and Karen would understand...eventually.

"Look out."

As they rounded a curve in the highway, a traffic jam stretched as far as they could see. Leo shifted down, pressed on the clutch, and then hit the brake. The Jeep came to a grinding stop inches from the semi-truck in front of them.

"You okay?" Leo asked Luke, his breathing ragged.

"Yeah, you?"

Leo could only nod.

"I'm going to find out what's going on." Luke got out and approached the truck ahead of them. He returned a few minutes later and shook his head. "The truck driver radioed a buddy up ahead. There's a bad accident about a mile away. Traffic is closed on both sides."

Leo picked up his cell phone and found no signal. "You got a signal?"

Luke checked his phone and shook his head. "No."

"We must be in a dead zone," Leo said. Which was where he'd be with Karen if he didn't get out of this mess.

»»•««

Karen did up the clasp of the amethyst necklace and stood back from the mirror. She really did look like a midnight Cinderella. How Leo had gotten her measurements for the dress and heels remained a mystery, one she'd get him to confess someday.

The thought of having a future with Leo put a smile on her face as she placed her curling iron back on the bathroom counter and examined her long loose curls. Perfect. For earrings she chose solitary diamonds, which she slipped on before grabbing her black cape and heading downstairs to wait for Robert.

She had the house to herself, as Mike and Geoff left an hour ago for a night of dinner and dancing. Karen had a feeling Mike wouldn't be a bachelor for much longer, and that thought made her smile...until she noticed the mess in the living room.

For the love of, she mumbled under her breath as she scooped up the innumerable TV remotes and put them in a basket. She swiped crumbs off the couch cushions before stopping to look at the picture of Emily she'd left on the coffee table. Emily didn't have Leo's dark hair, but they shared the same eyes and nose. Karen wondered what tragedy had taken this lovely, carefree girl away from her family. She also wondered why Leo had sent her this particular picture.

Tonight would be a night for answers, whether she liked them or not. Her stomach churned in response to her nervousness. Seeing him again after these two days apart would wreak havoc on her body and her heart. She needed her mind to be in top form, as she had more in store tonight than confronting Leo.

The doorbell rang. Karen checked her reflection in the mirror and then opened the door for Robert.

"Good evening, mademoiselle."

"Good evening, Robert. How are you?"

"I am well, and you look absolutely divine."

Karen's cheeks burned pleasantly from the compliment. "You are too sweet."

"Come, let's get your coat on and get you into the limo where it is nice and warm. I have some champagne on ice for you as well—to help with the nerves."

"You think of everything."

Robert bowed his head in thanks then proffered his arm to escort her to the limo. "Here we go," she whispered under her breath.

The drive to downtown wasn't as bad as Karen thought, but as they got closer to the venue traffic came to a standstill. "What's going on, Robert?" Karen asked as she tried to see out the tinted window.

"It's not the ideal venue, Ms. Karen. There is no parking and the snow is slowing everything down."

"So it would seem. Did you want me to get out and walk?"

"Definitely not. And Master Leo would have my head."

Karen sank back against the soft leather seat. "Where is Leo? Am I supposed to meet him inside?"

"Yes. I will get you there as quickly as I can, but you might miss the award ceremony."

"I've no interest in that."

"Well, then sit back and enjoy your bubbly, Ms. Karen. Can I put on some music for you?"

Karen nodded and took a sip from her glass. She had to admit the champagne was going to her head quite fast, as she'd forgotten to eat. She checked her cell phone for the umpteenth time then sent Kim a text. Kim texted back immediately saying the award ceremony was almost finished and there'd be some dancing before the fashion show. Karen's fingers flew across the keyboard. *Is Ms. Vale there?*

She was. Haven't seen her in a while.

Weird. *Is Mr. St. Clare there?*

No. Haven't seen him yet.

A feeling of dread filled her. The rational side of her knew the place was packed and Kim may have missed him. But her sensitive side hurt one too many times couldn't help being suspicious of the fact Leo and Natasha were nowhere to be found.

She could feel the limo inching forward and started going stir-crazy. When Robert stopped for a group of people crossing the street, Karen flung the door open and stepped out. Robert's yells faded when she slammed the door shut and rushed to the sidewalk.

There were people everywhere, laughing and shouting. One man played guitar for a small group of giggling women dressed seductively, with fur stoles wrapped around their bare shoulders. Karen averted her eyes whenever someone looked at her, and she quickened her pace. She could see the entrance to The Attic and the long lineup snaked around the corner.

Her stomach churned again, and nausea rose to her throat. By the time she got inside, she'd have missed everything. Stopping in the middle of the sidewalk, she texted Kim again.

I'm right outside. The line isn't moving.

Check with security. Most of those people are waiting to see celebrities come out and don't have invites.

Karen gave a sigh of relief and tightened her cape before heading closer. She'd barely taken a step when she noticed three men eyeing her and making their way closer. She took another step forward and felt a hand grabbing her shoulder from behind.

"Let go of me." Karen shouted, and she flung her arms in the air.

"Ms. Karen, it's me."

Robert turned her around, and Karen stared at him for a few seconds before placing her forehead on his chest. "Oh my God, Robert. You scared me half to death."

"What were you thinking, leaving the limo?" He berated her.

"I need to get inside."

"And you will—"

"Where is Leo?"

"Miss?"

"I have a friend inside who hasn't seen him all evening. Is he with Natasha Vale?"

"Oh, no. He hasn't seen her since she was at the condo the other night."

If she hadn't already been cold, she surely would've felt all the colour drain from her face. She'd been a fool to believe, yet again, Leo had changed. She checked her phone again, but no messages from him flashed up. When her phone vibrated in her hand, her heart leapt, but it was Kim.

I see you. Come on.

"I've got to go, Robert. My friend is waiting for me."

"I will escort you."

Remembering the men who were hovering nearby, she nodded her consent. Kim was standing beside the security guard, bouncing on her toes to keep warm. Karen kissed Robert on the cheek and said her thanks, and then Kim grabbed her hand and pulled her inside the stifling hot lobby of The Attic.

Body-pulsing music filled the room as they slowly made their way to the coat check.

"You look amazing," Kim praised when Karen turned around.

Karen's smile was genuine. "Thank you." She took in Kim's loose, flowing pink gown then gave her a hug. "Your dress is smashing."

"It hides imperfections."

"There is nothing to hide yet. You models are too picky."

Kim shrugged. "Wanna grab a drink?"

Karen did want to drink but shook her head. "Is there any food?"

"Oh, yes. A great buffet in the next room."

"Is Richard here yet?"

"He's been here since six."

"Good."

Kim's phone buzzed and her smile disappeared. "Oh no."

"What's wrong?"

"Ms. Vale's here."

"Are you working for her tonight?"

"Yes."

"Then you better get back there pronto. I'll find Richard and make sure everything is good to go. Remember, we're the last entry."

If Natasha was there then there was a good chance Leo was as well, Karen thought. She grabbed a small plate of food from the buffet and started mingling. Robert had been right; it wasn't the best venue for a fashion event in the middle of winter. In the summer, though, it would be gorgeous outside on the deck, with all the glimmering lights from the surrounding skyscrapers.

Tonight, propane fire pits were lit and plotted out at intervals to keep the heat under the tall canopy that shielded them from snow and wind. Surprised at how many people were actually outside, Karen walked out to be greeted with comfortable warmth and not the stuffy heat from the people dancing inside.

She made her way to the ledge on the far side of the deck, but her body shook from the cold. There were no fires there. She grabbed a glass of white wine from the waiter and brought it to her lips. Her nose wrinkled from the sourness, and she decided to try another sip.

The taste did improve with each sip she took, and soon the glass was empty. *Dammit.*

Another full glass of white wine appeared before her. "Can I join you this time?" a deep voice asked.

Leo stood beside her like a dream. His amber eyes glowed, and his hair shone jet black in the glittering chandelier light. The charcoal suit and silver shirt he wore seemed ready to burst open at his chest and shoulders. The long jacket hid his buttocks, but the pants were form-fitting and went on forever. He was her midnight Prince Charming, and he oozed gorgeousness.

Reining in her lust, Karen set a steely glare on Leo as all her insecurities rushed to the surface. Even though he was there and safe, she'd never felt more vulnerable or exposed, and she hated him for that.

She did the only thing she could think of to stem the green monster that grew inside her. She threw the contents of her wine glass into Leo's face.

»»•««

"Bloody hell, Karen."

Karen snatched a napkin from a nearby table and passed it to him.

"Sorry," she said. "Bad taste to do that when you look so hot."

Leo choked back a laugh as he wiped the liquid from his face. At least she'd had a good aim. Only the front of his suit was damp. "I'm sure I deserved it."

Karen tilted her chin and nodded. He noticed a slight tremble in her features and took a deep, calming breath.

"You look absolutely breathtaking. Better than I ever imagined."

The blush in her cheeks enhanced her beauty, and he wanted nothing more than to take her in his arms.

"If I get you another drink, do you promise not to throw it at me?"

"Yes, I promise."

Leo lifted two wine glasses off a passing waiter's tray and handed one to Karen. Lifting his glass up, he tilted it to touch the rim of hers in a toast but said nothing. What was there to say that didn't sound like an excuse or manipulation?

He had so much to say and no idea where to begin. Perhaps asking why he got wine in the face was as good a place as any.

"It's been a long time since a woman threw alcohol in my face."

"I'm sure it won't be the last."

Leo laughed. "Probably not."

Karen was shivering uncontrollably now. He removed his jacket and placed it over her shoulders. "That's sexy. Like a tuxedo dress."

"Oh, no. I forgot." Karen put her glass on the table and made a beeline for the door.

Leo caught up and grabbed her elbow. "Karen, where are you going?

"Backstage."

"I don't think that's a good idea."

Karen paused and bit her lower lip. Oh, how he wanted to kiss those lips. They did such naughty, wonderful things to his body.

"You're probably right. Can you go for me?"

Leo arched his brow in suspicion. "Why?" He dragged out the syllable.

"I need you to find Kim, who will find Richard, and bring them to me."

"What's going on?"

"You'll see soon enough."

"Karen—"

"It's a surprise."

"And if Nat interferes with this surprise?"

Karen's steely stare returned. "I'm sure you'll think of something to keep her occupied."

Leo found his way backstage easily, but not without having to stop and chat with almost everyone he passed. He had never craved the quiet life more than he did in that moment.

The chaos continued when he turned the corner: racks of clothing everywhere, models in chairs getting their hair and makeup done, and Nat yelling orders. He had to find Kim before Nat reeled him into working.

He dashed behind a clothes rack and made his way to the far corner of the room, where he found Kim hiding behind a pillar.

"Hey, Kim."

Relief flooded Kim's face. "Mr. St. Clare, I'm so glad to see you. Ms. Allen is looking for you."

"She's sent me to fetch you and Richard."

"I can't get him away from Ms. Vale."

"He does know about Karen's little surprise, doesn't he?"

"Yes, and he's trying, but she keeps calling him back."

He wouldn't be able to avoid Nat after all. "Looks like I'm cutting in. Meet Richard in the next room. Ms. Allen is on the deck."

"Okay."

Leo weaved his way through clothes and models and found Richard altering a sea-foam blue mermaid gown.

"Richard?"

"Ah, Mr. St. Clare. Good to see you again so soon. How does Ms. Allen like the dress?"

Leo looked around to make sure Nat was occupied elsewhere. "She looks amazing in it...but you need to go right now. Kim is waiting for you outside, and Karen is on the deck."

"You've come to relieve me then. Ms. Vale will not be happy if I disappear."

"I'll make sure she doesn't even notice." Leo scooped up the dress and blocked the way as Richard left.

Natasha spotted him right away. "Leo? What a surprise having you back here." She noticed the dress in his arms and frowned. "Isn't that the dress Richard is supposed to be working on?"

"It is. He handed it to me. He said it's ready to go, and he went to the little boys' room."

"Okay...well, you've taken Richard's job for the time being then. I need you to pin the skirt back on this dress...and where the hell is Kim?" she shouted to the room at large.

The DJ's announcement that the fashion show was about to begin boomed across the room. Nat went into instant wicked witch mode, and the room erupted into full-scale chaos. Leo got swept up in the excitement as model after model was ushered onto the stage. Before he knew it, the last model exited the stage and the DJ's voice boomed out again.

"We have one final entry and she's hot, hot, hot. Welcome back Kim, who is wearing an original design by independent designer Karen Allen."

Leo dashed out of the room in time to see Kim walking down the runway in a gorgeous floor-length gown that resembled a tuxedo. Feminine and airy, the skirt flowed in perfect folds against Kim's legs. The sleeves, in a sheer black, ended at the wrist with a thick white cuff and black diamond cufflinks. The pièce de résistance was a white collar and lapel. All in all, it was a work of art.

The room erupted in applause. Pride swelled in his chest and love filled his heart. Karen had done it. She'd broken into the designer scene and was a hit. Eager to congratulate her, Leo started to make his way through the crowd. He was only a few feet away when he heard Nat's voice rise above the chattering of the crowd.

"How dare you sneak in here with this?" Her tone oozed with disgust. "You are a lowly intern and know nothing about design. You copied it like you did that sketch."

Chapter 11

Karen crashed from the high of applause and congratulations when Natasha hurled those lies for everyone to hear.

"This is my design. Always has been," Karen defended.

Natasha looked around at her peers and laughed. "Can you believe her? An intern trying to come off as a designer. As one of those who work endless hours creating art."

"I'm no longer an intern."

"That's right. I fired your incompetent ass." Natasha addressed the crowd again. "Trust me when I say she's the worst assistant I've ever had."

"We don't need to do this here," Karen said so only Natasha could hear.

"Yes, we do." Natasha flicked her hair over her shoulder and let out a fake laugh.

"No, we don't. You don't like me, you're jealous, and now you want to embarrass me in front of the industry. I am not going to play your little game."

"This is no game." Natasha retorted. "You have no proof this design is yours. I have the—"

Karen smiled. "The sketch I dropped that Stacey picked up and you claimed was a copy?"

"I don't know what you mean." Natasha backed up a few inches.

"Have you even looked at that sketch since you tucked it away in your desk drawer?"

"Yes, I have. I—"

"It doesn't resemble anything close to the design you saw tonight. Kim, come here a minute, please."

Kim descended the few steps off the stage, and the crowd let her through to Karen's side. "In the sketch the dress is knee length and the sleeves are short. The beginnings of a rough draft I'd barely spent half an hour on. This creation," Karen paused to sweep her hands down the dress in a grand fashion, "is my design. It's what I've been working on in every spare moment I've had, and I have the pattern here with me if you or anyone wants to challenge me. I'm here tonight to show you, to show the fashion world that I'm more than an intern who fetches coffee and picks up dry cleaning."

The crowd's mumbling grew louder. Karen couldn't tell if they were for or against her, but she didn't care. She'd come into her own, and her design had been well received by the industry representatives gathered there.

Turning to face the crowd, Karen raised her voice so she could be heard. "Thank you so much for allowing me to participate in this show, this amazing week..." Tears formed in the corners of her eyes. "Thank you." The whisper barely left her lips before Kim squealed with joy and then enveloped her in a bear hug. The crowd burst into applause. Out of the corner of her eye, Karen saw Natasha stomp off. Then she saw Leo standing by the stage with the biggest grin on his face. Like Emily's.

It occurred to her at that moment that she didn't need Leo to protect her or to have her back. She'd found the courage and the confidence to succeed on her own...with the help of some good friends.

Before she knew it, she was bombarded with congratulations. *Oh, what a night.*

»»·««

Leo finally found Karen alone an hour later around one of the fire pits on the deck. The crowd had started to thin out, but the DJ had turned on the tunes for the last few stragglers who weren't ready to leave yet.

"Hey," Leo said as he walked closer.

Karen looked up and smiled, but it didn't quite reach her eyes.

"Hey."

"You had an amazing night." He stood across from her and stuck out his hands for the fire to keep warm.

"It went better than I'd hoped."

"Congratulations."

"Thanks."

He didn't say anything for a long while as he drank in the view of her in that dress. She had a black cape on now, but the contrast of her blonde hair against the dark cloth only enhanced her beauty. Her skin glowed from the cold, but her eyes were wary and tired.

"I'm sorry I wasn't here to meet you as planned."

"I should've known better." Her gaze never left the fire.

Leo's breath caught in surprise at the emptiness of her tone. Had she given up on him for good? He needed to explain. She had to listen. He hoped she'd hear him.

"We went to the winery today," Leo blurted out in his nervousness, his hands back in his pockets.

"Oh, so you're a 'we' now?"

"Walter and Bea returned from a market run last night and I wanted to show— What?"

"Nothing." She rubbed her hands together and continued to stare into the flames.

It dawned on him who she thought had gone to the winery with him.

"Karen, look at me." He took hold of her hands over the fire. "Please."

Karen looked up; her gaze wary.

"Luke and I went to the winery."

Confusion filled her gaze. "Luke? Your brother?"

"Yes."

A long pause followed. He watched the play of emotions on her face, from confusion to relief to anger.

"Why didn't you call me?" she asked as she pulled her hands out of his grasp.

"There was a bad car accident and the highway was blocked on both sides. I tried to call but we were in a dead zone." Karen didn't look convinced. "I promise. Check your phone."

"It died a few hours ago."

"Oh."

"And what about Natasha?" she asked, her arms wrapped protectively around her middle. "I heard she was at your condo the other night."

Leo gulped back the lump that had formed in his throat. "She came by while I was trying to nurse my hangover."

"And?"

"And...she hit on me."

Karen's fists were clenched at her sides and her lips quivered. "Leo, I need to know."

"There's nothing going on between us. We are old high school friends."

"I don't think she feels the same way."

He recalled Natasha's provocative touch and how she'd made herself at home. "No. I don't believe so either."

"I don't want to be an emotional mess, but my heart can't take anymore pain. Natasha is always flirting and bragging about the two of you. Insinuating more than what's on the surface. And you are so cryptic, not really giving me a yes or no."

"But I told you."

"A little too late."

"Karen, please." Leo felt nauseous. He'd dug a deeper hole than he'd realised. She didn't trust him with her most important possession: her heart.

"And you were never there for me when I needed support or to have my back when she was bullying me."

"I wasn't going to fight your battles for you."

"I wasn't asking you to. I needed you to care and be there for me to lean on. I didn't have anyone to rely on in my teen years when the bullying was at its worst. My parents were old-fashioned and unapproachable, and I don't have any siblings... I thought I'd at least have you now."

"Why didn't you tell me how bad the bullying was before?"

"Same reason you didn't tell me about your sister."

"I don't think—"

"I didn't want to rehash the past, or for you to think I am weak."

"I've never thought that about you. Ever."

Karen shrugged off the comment and continued. "The bullying stopped after I graduated high school but being at Vale Designs has brought all the memories back. Amazing how your confidence can take such a blow and putting it back together again can be the hardest thing to do."

He'd been a self-absorbed idiot. "I'm so sorry." He looked up at her, but her focus was on the fire. "Can I tell you about Emily?"

"You don't have to tell me." Karen's voice dripped with sarcasm.

Ouch. He deserved that. "I want to tell you."

Karen nodded but kept her eyes averted.

"I've done a lot of soul searching since my drunken episode the other day. I've been haunted by my past for way too long and not letting anyone in...not letting you in. I confronted Luke yesterday. I'm afraid he took the brunt of my pent-up anger and guilt, but he didn't throw it back in my face or blame me. I started to see things from a different perspective...from my family's perspective, and a heavy weight was lifted. It was a relief to begin letting go of the guilt I've carried for the past ten years."

Karen stepped a bit closer, watching him intently now. "Why did you wait so long to talk to them about Emily?"

Leo's pulse was racing so fast his heart felt like it would burst through his ribcage. He felt a light sweat form on his forehead and upper lip. Other than to Luke, he'd never said the words out loud.

"I, umm...I'm the reason..." Leo took a deep breath and looked Karen in the eyes. Patience and kindness had replaced the anger and hurt of only moments ago.

"I'm the reason Emily is dead."

Karen gasped but didn't move away. "I don't believe that."

"I couldn't save her." Leo closed his eyes, and his mind drifted back to that day when he'd pulled her out of the pool and tried resuscitating her. His girlfriend at the time had been there and called the ambulance. But they'd lived on an estate in the countryside, so the ambulance couldn't reach them in time. Emily was gone.

"My parents had left me in charge of Emily yet again as they went gallivanting across Europe in their never-ending quest to expand the wine business."

Leo looked up but didn't really see anything but the past that replayed in his mind. "I was eighteen years old and tired of being stuck playing babysitter to a ten-year-old instead of having fun with my friends." He took a deep breath. "I was in the house making out with my girlfriend instead of watching Emily. She told me she was going swimming, and all I said was 'Yeah yeah, get out of here.' Those were my last words to her."

Karen took Leo in her embrace. Her arms were strong around him, and he welcomed the warmth. He couldn't stop the overwhelming roller coaster of sadness that started in his belly and crept up to his heart and then his throat. A huge sob escaped, and he buried his face in Karen's shoulder.

Her embrace tightened even more, if that was possible. She ran her hand up and down his back in a soothing motion. He'd never received such love, not even from his parents.

Leo stepped away but held onto her shoulders.

"I have a lot of things to work out. I'm going to see a counsellor. Luke and my parents, as well. We have a lot of healing to do."

"Counselling is a big step in the right direction. I'm proud of you." Her smile wobbled under his gaze, but her strength shined through like a beacon of hope.

"Thank you."

Karen ran her hands along his jacket lapels. "I—"

Kim called out Karen's name. They turned to see her standing near the entrance. "You ready to go?" Kim asked.

Karen nodded then turned to Leo and gently touched his cheek. Her eyes shone with unshed tears. "Go and heal. You deserve to be happy."

She stepped back then walked away. Leo reached out, but she was already halfway across the deck. "Karen..."

She joined Kim at the door and then turned to face him. "Take care of yourself."

And she was gone.

»»·««

Karen picked up a purring Charlie and carried him out to the back deck of her childhood home. Anna sat on the porch swing with a cup of coffee in her hand watching Jace as he showed their new baby boy, Nikolas, all the blooming flowers in the garden.

"He's only two weeks old and already getting the gardening lecture," Anna said with a smile of pure contentment.

"Be glad it's that and not real estate mumbo jumbo."

Anna laughed and moved over so Karen could sit. "I think that's next week's lecture." Karen sat beside Anna and pulled a blanket over her legs to shield herself from the morning chill. Charlie kneaded her lap for a few minutes before finally settling in for a nap, and Karen stroked his soft fur as she looked out at the yard enjoying the view of early buds on the trees and listening to the birds chirping. It was good to be home.

"Thank you for looking after my fur baby for me."

"He was no trouble at all. If anything, he was a little too clingy, weren't you buddy?" Anna rubbed under his chin, and he meowed his response.

Home for a month now, Karen had enjoyed the time spent catching up with her best friend and loved being an auntie to baby Nikolas. Otherwise, she'd been keeping her mind occupied working on a few new pieces to go along with her tuxedo dress.

Anna took a sip of her coffee. "You know, Ms. Tallon wants you back at *Dogwood*."

No spark of excitement jostled in her tummy at the offer. "I don't know if I can go back to the business side of things. I've got the design bug."

"I know all about that."

"You've taught me so much and been so patient with all my questions and freak-outs."

"I'll always be there for you."

Karen turned to envelop Anna in a sideways hug. "Thank you."

A few moments of comfortable silence passed. A horn honked in the distance, and a flock of geese flew overhead. Jace's voice drifted toward them from the garden. He really did know a lot about flowers.

"Any word from Leo?" Anna asked, turning in her seat to face Karen.

Karen concentrated on rubbing Charlie's belly now that he'd flipped over. "No. And why would I? I let him go."

"Only so he and his family could heal. It was a selfless thing you did."

"It hurts so bad," Karen said, afraid if she spoke louder, she'd burst into tears. She loved him, true and fully. There was no denying it any longer. If she was truthful with herself, she'd loved him all along.

Charlie's purr turned to a low hum, and Karen closed her eyes. She couldn't stop thinking of Leo and all the pain he'd lived with for so long. Choosing to suffer alone... Her heart ached so bad for him—for them.

His distance with her five years ago made sense now, as she recalled asking him lots of questions about his family that he'd refused to answer. She'd kept bringing up the painful memories he'd been trying to run from, and instead of confronting them, he'd run one more time...out of her life.

The glimpse into his childhood that he'd revealed at the gala had also given her a clearer picture of the man he'd become. To push down the guilt and memories, he'd lived his life at top speed, with no cares or consequences. Would he continue that lifestyle after his counselling sessions? She really hoped not.

Charlie let out a loud meow, and Karen opened her eyes. "What's going on, buddy?" Karen stroked his head, but he meowed again, louder this time. A deck board squeaked, and Karen turned in her seat, causing Charlie to jump down and run into the yard.

Anna stood, and Jace zipped around the corner with Nikolas in his arms.

Leo was standing a few feet away looking pale and a bit dishevelled, with a day's worth of beard growth on his face and dark circles under his eyes.

"Hello." His deep voice raised goose bumps on Karen's arms, and she shivered.

She stood, and the blanket fell to the ground. "Hi."

Leo pointed his thumb at the house. "I...um...the front door was open."

"No problem."

Nikolas started to fuss, and Anna went to him. Jace took her hand. "We should go."

Anna nodded. "Karen, we'll talk to you later."

"Okay." She watched them walk around the side of the house, where a gate led to the front yard.

Karen turned back. "That was my best friend, Anna, her husband, Jace, and their new baby, Nikolas."

"They are a beautiful family."

"Yes, they are."

They stared at each other for a long moment then Leo moved closer. "How have you been?"

"Busy." She wanted to say 'miserable'. "You?"

"Busy. I've done a month's worth of counselling sessions."

"Good."

"We're nowhere near done," he blurted out.

"I know." Karen smiled at his nervousness.

"But I did work through the most important issue in my life right now."

Karen's breath caught then turned shallow. "Which is?"

Leo moved even closer, so their hips were touching, and their lips were only an inch apart. "You."

Karen exhaled her pent-up breath. "Me?"

"My counsellor told me I need to be happy with my life right now in order to fix the past."

"Sound advice."

"He asked what my heart's desire is."

"And?" Karen's body burned pleasantly from the closeness of his. She wanted to embrace him; to kiss his lips until neither of them could breathe.

"I bought the B&B."

Karen's eyes widened in surprise and her stomach churned, but she forced a smile on her face. "I knew you would."

"And I want to construct a new addition in the back, facing the vineyard, where my wife can spend her days creating her own clothing line that will knock the New York fashion world off its feet."

"You...your...wife?"

Leo bent down on one knee and took her hand. "Karen, will you marry me?"

Karen froze. She couldn't think or make her lips move. Leo stood and took her other hand. He didn't appear fazed at all by her lack of response.

"I love you. I always have. You ground me in the chaotic world I created for myself, which I want no part of now."

A single tear escaped and ran down her cheek. Leo wiped it away with such gentleness that another tear followed.

"By tackling your fears and demons, you showed me how to persevere through my own issues, and I would have no one else by my side as I continue that journey."

Karen let out a small sob and covered her mouth with her hands. Tears streamed down her cheeks in full force now.

"So, Ms. Allen, will you marry me, then live out our days together at the B&B while you design clothes to your heart's content?"

Karen nodded and then pulled Leo closer. She kissed him with such passion that they were both panting when the kiss ended.

"Is that a yes?" Leo asked. His eyes held a trace of doubt.

"Oh, yes," Karen said, and she kissed Leo again. "Looks like I've tamed the lion." Her amber-eyed lion.

"That you did." Leo laughed. "Thank goodness."

Karen ran her hand down his stubbled cheek, her gaze intent on his. "I love you...so much. I didn't think I'd see you again when I walked away in New York. But I knew you needed time to start your healing process with your family, and if that meant not being with you..."

"We're together now," Leo said, and he kissed her lips lightly. "And this isn't a one-way street. I'm here for you now, if you need me to be. Always."

His words meant more to Karen than she'd ever thought possible.

"I need you," Karen said. Charlie came back on the deck and rubbed against Leo's legs. "Well, you've got Charlie's seal of approval. Welcome to the family."

Leo bent over to pet Charlie's head and then took Karen's hand. "I told Robert he'd be the first to know your answer."

"Robert's here?"

Leo nodded. "He's waiting in the town car I rented."

"He's been an amazing rock of support for you, hasn't he?"

"The best. He's more like a father figure to me, and I really don't know where I'd be without him."

The two of them really did have a great support system of family and friends, Karen realised. She couldn't wait to start the next adventure in their lives. It was going to be a doozy.

Leo smiled. "It'll definitely be that."

Acknowledgements

I want to thank my publisher and editor Annabel Townsend for believing in me and my stories; for her endless hours formatting, answering my questions, and making last minute changes to help bring my vision to life.

To Meredith Hughes for designing my new amazing cover; I love how it hints at the story through photographs.

I am grateful to my friend Erin Hamel for brainstorming with me and reading various versions to help get my story to where it is today.

Thank you to my husband Chris for his unwavering support and belief in me, to my sons Nicholas and Clark for being so supportive, kind, and the best cheerleaders.

To Amanda and the staff at Bar Willow Eatery in Regina for the best Dining in the Dark experience. I enjoyed comparing my experience with Karen and Leo's at Les Sens in New York. Les Sens is an imaginary restaurant but takes after the real *Abigail's Kitchen* Dining in the Dark Experience. Visit these links to learn the differences:

www.abigailskitchennyc.com/dinners-in-the-dark

https://www.facebook.com/BarWillowEatery

And a big thank you to all my readers for the kind comments and reviews that you leave for me. I am so lucky and honoured to share my stories with you.

About the Author

Tricia Saxby is from Regina, born and raised. Having spent the last 16 years raising their two boys in Kamloops, BC, she and her husband moved home, new empty-nesters and fuzzy kid parents to a sassy cat and a high-energy puppy.

Working in the medical field as a transcriptionist for her whole career, Tricia spent her free time reading and writing romance stories. Since then, she's written and published short stories in five anthologies and a six-sentence blogspot, and has professional certifications in line-editing and proofreading.

When not working or writing/editing, Tricia enjoys taking her puppy for walks, crocheting purses, or sitting on her deck enjoying a glass of wine and a good book.

Her Ex's Secret is part of Tricia's duet of romance books, with the second part due to be published in early 2025.